ZURI DAY

SIN CITY VOWS

D0186931

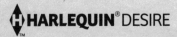

HARLEQUIN® DESIRE

Recycling programs
for this product may
not exist in your area.

ISBN-13: 978-1-335-60353-1

Sin City Vows

Copyright © 2019 by Zuri Day

All rights reserved. Except for use in any review, the reproduction or
utilization of this work in whole or in part in any form by any electronic,
mechanical or other means, now known or hereafter invented, including
xerography, photocopying and recording, or in any information storage
or retrieval system, is forbidden without the written permission of the
publisher, Harlequin Enterprises Limited, 22 Adelaide St. West, 40th Floor,
Toronto, ON M5H 4E3, Canada.

This is a work of fiction. Names, characters, places and incidents are
either the product of the author's imagination or are used fictitiously,
and any resemblance to actual persons, living or dead, business
establishments, events or locales is entirely coincidental.

This edition published by arrangement with Harlequin Books S.A.

For questions and comments about the quality of this book,
please contact us at CustomerService@Harlequin.com.

® and TM are trademarks of Harlequin Enterprises Limited or its
corporate affiliates. Trademarks indicated with ® are registered in the
United States Patent and Trademark Office, the Canadian Intellectual
Property Office and in other countries.

Printed in U.S.A.

Lauren braced herself against the onslaught of desire.

When their eyes connected, she felt girlie, almost shy, and the silky kimono mini that draped her body teased her skin. An unbidden image flashed through her mind—Christian's lips replacing the fabric that kissed her skin.

As quickly as it appeared, she shut her mind against it.

Christian was a tempting morsel. He was also Victoria's eldest born and Lauren had no plans to get entangled with the boss's son.

"Good evening, Lauren."

She nodded slightly. "Christian."

Christian paused, looked around. "Is this your handiwork?"

"I had help."

His eyes narrowed, darkened as they shifted from the room's decor to Lauren's face. An expression as tantalizing as it was unreadable sent a blast of heat to her core.

What was it about this guy, she wondered, that lit her body up like a match?

* * *

Sin City Vows is part of the
Sin City Secrets series from Zuri Day.

Dear DayDreamer,

Have you ever had a disappointing experience, only to later realize what happened was a blessing in disguise? Or been heartbroken over losing a "great" guy who was really a jerk, eventually learning you dodged a bullet? Or what about situations where others felt they knew better for you than you knew for yourself? If you can relate, then you'll identify with Lauren Hart, a woman determined to live life on her own terms.

I could really relate to Lauren and her struggle to exist in her own authenticity, even when it wasn't popular or was a little bit uncomfortable. Even when doing so felt risky, a throw of the dice. It helped to have a sexy distraction like Christian Breedlove to smooth out some of the rough patches and give her a different perspective. She never would have dreamed that a preteen crush would come full circle. Life's like that. Just when we think we've got it all figured out, we get zapped by the unexpected. And sometimes, that which we never considered ends up being the best thing that could have ever happened. Better than we could have dreamed.

Enjoy, and have a zuriday.com!

Zuri

Zuri Day is the national bestselling author of two dozen novels, including the popular Drakes of California series. She is a winner of the RSJ Emma Award, the AALAS (African American Literary Awards Show) Best Romance Award and others, and a finalist for multiple *RT Book Reviews* Best Book Awards in Multicultural Fiction. She wants you to have a zuriday.com!

Books by Zuri Day

Harlequin Desire

Sin City Secrets
Sin City Vows

Harlequin Kimani Romance

Champagne Kisses
Platinum Promises
Solid Gold Seduction
Secret Silver Nights
Crystal Caress

Visit her Author Profile page at Harlequin.com, or zuriday.com, for more titles.

For all of us who've dreamed of vows
Experienced love's oohs and aahs and wows
The journey is worth it but not always pretty
As you'll see in this read that takes place in Sin City

One

Breedlove birthdays were always exciting. As the first-born son of this close-knit clan, Christian knew that well. But as he relaxed against the company limo's luxurious interior, he had to give it to the family, especially his dad. They'd surprised him at a time in his life when he thought few things could. The gift he'd received just hours ago had been totally unexpected, had humbled the self-confident, almost cocky businessman in him even as it had filled him with pride.

Now, as they passed the family mansion and reached the estate's private airstrip, Christian realized one more surprise awaited him. A slow smile spread across his face, highlighting dimples that more than a few times had gotten him out of trouble with authority and into the romantic crosshairs of the opposite sex. One look and he was mesmerized. What he saw was a thing of beauty. Sleek lines, muted earth tones, curves in all the right places. *Wow*.

Christian looked over at his brother Adam, who was on his smartphone, texting away. "You knew about this?"

Adam looked up. "About what?"

Christian's smile broadened. "Yeah, you knew about it. Ty is here." His best friend had cut short his business trip and come to help the eldest Breedlove sibling celebrate a milestone. And boy, had he arrived in style.

The sound of another car approaching pulled Christian away from the dazzling view. He turned and saw his dad's newest toy—a black Escalade SUV customized with all the bells and whistles—pull up next to the limo that he'd exited. Their driver, Elvis, hopped out and opened the door for Christian's mother, Victoria, while his father, Nicholas, eased out the other back door, grinning as he approached his firstborn.

They knew about this, too? That Tyson had flown in to surprise him on his birthday and show off what looked to be a brand-new Gulfstream G600 jet?

"Well, son, what do you think?"

Christian returned his attention to the rare and opulent beauty now backlit by the setting sun.

"I think I owe Tyson money."

"Why?" Adam had finally put away his phone when they pulled up and exited the limo to join the group.

"To settle a bet. After flying in one of those customized babies last year, we put a thousand bucks on which one of us would be the first to get our own." Christian waved his hand toward the plane. "Looks like Ty won."

The door of the plane opened. Christian took a step forward as the airstair lowered and someone moved through the doorway.

"Happy birthday, Christian."

He stopped in his tracks, shielding his eyes against the sunlight to get a better view of the newcomer, convinced that the ethereal beauty before him could not be real. A woman—tall, richly tanned, with curly dark hair cascading over one shoulder—beckoned him with a smile.

Stunned, Christian turned to his mother, who now stood next to Nicholas, her face beaming. "Who is that?"

"You remember Lauren, don't you, dear? Faye's daughter? She was heading this way, and I felt you wouldn't mind that she caught a ride on your plane."

"Wait, *what*? My…" Christian looked from his parents to Adam. Everyone was smiling.

Nicholas slapped Christian's back before placing an arm around his shoulders. "Happy birthday, son."

Christian turned back to where Lauren now descended the plane's airstair. She was dressed in a belted wide-legged jumpsuit that emphasized pert, ample breasts and a small, curvy waist, and Christian noted a casual yet almost regal air about the way she carried herself. The emerald color brought out the golden tones in her skin and highlighted specks of green in the hazel eyes now fixed on him as she neared them.

He whispered to his mother, almost incredulously, "Is that my birthday present?"

Victoria continued to smile at Lauren while coyly replying, "Only the plane, son." Seconds later Lauren stepped into her open arms. "Hello, darling."

"Hi, Victoria." Lauren turned to Christian. "Hi, Chris."

"Hello." He hitched a thumb toward the plane as he looked at her. "So, Tyson isn't in there?"

"Who's Tyson?" Lauren asked.

"Chris's best friend," Adam replied.

Lauren slowly shook her head from side to side. The impish upturn of plump, glossy lips begging to be kissed suggested to Christian that she'd been in on it, too.

He turned sincere, grateful eyes on his parents. "Mom, Dad… I don't know what to say except…wow…thanks."

"You deserve it, son," Nicholas said.

Christian turned back to the plane. "Well, hot damn!" he exclaimed as the truth fully sank in. He reached out and offered Lauren his arm, which she graciously accepted, then gestured for his family to follow them. "Come on, beautiful. Show me around!"

Even in his excitement, Christian noted Lauren's silky skin and caught the subtle scent of something floral and delectably spicy. Gentleman that he was, he stepped back and allowed her to precede him up the stairs. The view from the back was the same as from the front—very alluring. So much so that entering the upscale and stately cabin that had been tailor-made to the specific instructions of his interior designer mother was almost anticlimactic.

Almost, but not quite. As Christian stepped inside the cabin and looked around, the magnitude of his parents' generosity made his chest swell with gratitude. The interior was exactly what he'd imagined while talking with Tyson, as comfortable as any found in the homes on the Breedlove estate. Walls covered in ivory suede. Ebony-stained hardwood floors. Recliners upholstered in jacquard chenille boasting company colors of black, white and tan. Seats on the left side of the cabin could be swiveled to view the flat screen mounted up front or around to the dining table behind them.

Christian looked from Lauren to his mom, his voice raspy with emotion. "How did you know?"

"Your brother, sweetheart. Adam talked to Tyson not long after the two of you had the extensive custom jet conversation and made that wager."

"Tyson knew about this surprise?" Adam nodded. "And he kept his mouth shut, for almost a year?"

"Wonders never cease, bro," Adam replied.

The pilot came out of the cockpit. Christian recognized him at once. "Not you, too," Christian muttered, shaking the outstretched hand of the family friend who'd grown up with his father and now piloted the company plane. "Am I the only one who wasn't in on this secret?"

Nicholas nodded. "Just about."

"Allow me to show you around," the pilot offered. "She's a real beauty. Glad I got to fly her first."

Once again, Christian held out his arm. "Care to join me on the tour?"

Adam hooked his muscular forearm through the one Christian offered. "I'd love to."

Christian moved his brother aside and placed a hand on Lauren's back. "Do you have brothers?"

"No."

"Do you want one?" Her throaty chuckle was music to his ears. Nicholas and Victoria sat on the white leather sleeper sofa that anchored the right side of the cabin while Christian, Lauren and Adam checked out the accommodations. There was a granite bath with a full shower, a compact chef's kitchen, two sleeping bunks along with a master bedroom, and an area set up as a small private office but that had padded flooring and workout equipment hidden behind the walls.

"How'd she do, Chris?" Nicholas asked when the group returned to the front of the cabin. He stood, then turned to help Victoria up. "Your mom get the design just about right?"

"It's incredible," Christian said, moved. "It's everything I imagined and much more. Hard to wrap my brain around. Earlier this week, the promotion to president, I thought that was the gift."

"Speaking of..." Nicholas turned and removed a thin

layer of paper covering a platinum plaque with carved lettering: Christian Breedlove, President. CANN International Inc.

Christian took it in with the utmost pride. The acronym, CANN, stood for the names of him and his brothers—Christian, Adam, Noah and Nick—along with the family's unwavering belief that while working together there was nothing they couldn't do. That belief was the foundation of the Breedloves' empire, an international chain of casino hotels and spas that were second to none.

"That's…exquisite." He smiled and swallowed hard. "Where are the twins? Since everyone knew about it, the dynamic duo should be here, too."

"They're handling the second half of the evening." Victoria eyed her watch. "Dinner at the hotel, where we should be heading right about now. Hope you're hungry. Holding in the secret all day left me with very little appetite. Now that it's out, I'm starved."

Christian hugged his dad and mom and kissed her on the cheek. He shook Adam's hand before pulling him into a tight embrace.

"Jesse," Nicholas called out to the pilot. "You're welcome to join us."

"I've got a hot date," Jesse replied. "But thanks."

The group headed down the stairs and over to where the drivers leaned against the gleaming black limousine. Christian placed a hand on Lauren's arm until the others had taken several steps and created a bit of distance between them. He wanted to take a moment and properly thank her for participating in his birthday surprise. He knew with Adam in the limo he'd get in few words.

Adam saw the move and stopped, too. "I'll catch a ride with Mom and Dad. You two can take the limo."

"Thanks, bro," Christian said.

"Only because it's your birthday." He threw a playful punch at his brother and headed to the SUV.

Moments later, Christian and Lauren entered the limo. The driver followed the SUV's circuitous route out of the estate and across to Las Vegas Boulevard, where the CANN hotel anchored one end of the Strip.

"It appears I'm supposed to know you," Christian whispered once they'd settled into the roomy seats. "But that's impossible."

A slight arch of Lauren's manicured brow preceded her response. "Is it?"

"Absolutely. You look…ravishing. There's no way I'd forget having met you."

"Well, you did."

He thought for a moment. "You're Faye's daughter? Faye Hart?"

Lauren nodded. "Yes."

Christian liked Lauren's voice, low and husky. He could imagine how it would sound in the throes of passion as he branded her as his.

"It's been at least two years since I've seen her, so when did you and I meet?"

"When I was twelve, and just so you know, my inner child is wounded."

Lauren feigned a pout. Christian's eyes dropped to pursed lips now held tightly together. Even though he knew she was joking, he wanted to kiss her until the frown disappeared, and then kiss her some more.

Not sure he could touch those lips, though, and keep the kiss chaste, he reached out and squeezed her hand instead.

"Twelve?" Christian's relieved laugh was genuine. "Did you look then the way you do now?"

"Not quite." Lauren laughed, too. "I was four years

younger than my sister, Renee. You were all into her. I was practically invisible." Lauren delivered the last line with a whine appropriate for a jilted preteen.

Christian's head fell back as more laughter erupted. "Renee Hart! Now it's all coming back to me. You guys used to live in California but moved across the country to…"

"Maryland. My dad took a job in Washington, DC. They bought a home in nearby Brandywine."

"Right. That was part of the excuse used for my being rejected. I think she had a boyfriend. I didn't want to visit LA for a while after that. My sixteen-year-old ego was crushed." He placed his hand over his heart. "In remembering my anguish then, I can very much relate to your inner child's pain."

The atmosphere shifted as comfortable interaction morphed into daunting attraction. Christian opened the door to an elaborate minibar. "Would you like a drink?"

"No, thanks. I'm good."

"Come on, it's my birthday. Don't make me drink alone."

"Okay, champagne then."

Christian opened a bottle of pricey champagne and filled two flutes. He handed one to Lauren. Their fingers touched. Sparks. Heat. *Did she feel that?* He looked up. She glanced away.

Yes, she'd felt something.

"To what shall we toast?" he asked.

"You, of course. It's your birthday, and given your gift, it's obviously a big one."

"For a second back there I thought the plane belonged to a friend of mine, Tyson, and had the foolish hope that you were my present."

Her eyes narrowed in a face that became impossible to read. "A foolish hope, indeed."

Christian moaned. "My second try for a Hart girl…
rejected again."

"You can handle it." Lauren winked. "You're an old
man now."

"Indeed. The big three-o."

"Over the hill," Lauren joked.

"Totally."

"To your birthday," she said.

"And beautiful gifts," Christian added.

They clinked glasses and sipped.

"So…whatever happened to your sister and that guy?"

Lauren shrugged. "He probably got dumped, like all
the others. Until her senior year in college, when she met
the man who is now her husband and a father of two."

"Good for her." He set down the flute. "What about
you?"

"What about me?"

"I don't see a ring."

Lauren's hands flew up in a defensive position. "No,
and you won't."

"Dang, girl, you sound even more adamant than me."
Christian chuckled and lifted his glass. "To the single life."

"Hear, hear."

"So…why didn't Faye come with you to visit my
mom?"

"It's more than a visit. I'll be working here."

"Oh, you've relocated for work. Who with?"

"Victoria. I'm her new personal assistant. As I understand it, I'll work primarily on events for your family's
nonprofit organization."

A slightly raised brow was Christian's only reaction.
Inside, he felt a pang of disappointment. So much for the
thought of a one-night stand with Lauren, or a short-term
girlfriend to cuddle with during the cold winter months.

He didn't date women involved with family business. Directly or indirectly, anyone working with his mother was no longer fair game. Any other day he would have figured it out sooner. But that week's promotion, his birthday and the shockingly extravagant birthday gift had dimmed his awareness and caused him to be off guard.

However, now Lauren's presence was becoming crystal clear. His mother, Victoria the matchmaker, was at it again. It was no secret that she wanted him to settle down, get married and start a family. All of which were not high on his agenda. And then there was another darker thought. Maybe his mom wasn't matchmaking. Maybe Lauren was manipulating her. It wouldn't be the first time a woman had used Victoria's passion for helping others through the family's foundation as a way to get to him.

He sighed, settled against the car's supple leather seats and thoughtfully sipped his champagne. The possible truth behind Lauren's visit cleared away the ardent desire her appearance had first aroused. The last thing he needed was a potentially messy fling with the daughter of one of his mom's good friends. He'd just been promoted to president of a multibillion-dollar hotel, casino and spa conglomerate with properties on five continents. What he needed in a female companion was someone fun with no ulterior motives or long-term expectations. Right now, he was married to the family business, and for the foreseeable future, CANN International would be his only wife.

Two

He was sexier and more handsome than Lauren remembered. The teen who'd stolen her twelve-year-old heart and remained her secret crush all through high school. Tall, lean, sporting curly black hair in a clean, cropped cut that was shorter on the sides and fuller on top. The eyes were the same—dark, intense—and his magnetic smile still had the power to render her breathless.

Even after she'd begun dating, and throughout a fairly serious relationship that began in college and lasted four years, Lauren had loosely followed Christian, the Breedloves and CANN International's ever-expanding empire, which was often in the news. A few years ago the company made history by building the first seven-star hotel and casino in North America, a distinction given to them by *Top-Tier Travel Digest*, the bible for agents and others who catered to the wealthy, the world's 1-percenters and the 1 percent of the 1 percent.

Socially, Christian was a paparazzi favorite, often making the gossip columns and the tabloids while attending Hollywood premieres and high-society events with a gorgeous girl on his arm. Last year, when he made the coveted Thirty Under Thirty list, she'd bookmarked the online article and shared it with her sister Renee. Every year, the names were compiled by business industry legends who pegged the next group of savvy, successful businessmen on the rise, the ones to watch.

Christian was not only jaw-droppingly good-looking, but he was a smart, progressive thinker as well. Were she in the market for a boyfriend, the man seated beside her had all kinds of potential. But she wasn't looking, and especially not for someone like the almighty Christian Breedlove. Not wanting to be manipulated by a rich, powerful man was precisely why she'd fled the East Coast.

"How'd that happen?" Christian asked as the limo headed down the crowded Strip toward their final destination. "You deciding to move here to work for Mom?"

"Very quickly," Lauren said, hitching in a breath as they inched toward the CANN Casino, Hotel and Spa, an award-winning steel-and-glass masterpiece whose tallest point brushed the sky at almost fourteen hundred feet. "Just a day or so ago."

"Really, that fast?"

"Yes." She shifted her gaze back to his remarkably handsome face. "Victoria was venting to Mom about a dilemma. Her assistant resigned abruptly and gave no notice, in the middle of planning a Valentine's Day–themed fashion show and several springtime charity events that Victoria says are very important to the foundation's funding. Mom mentioned that she thought I could help, and Victoria called and asked if I could come over ASAP. I understand the fashion show is just a week away and is a very big deal."

Christian nodded, thoughtfully rubbing his chin. "Speaking of abrupt notices, what about your employer?"

"She was totally understanding." To his raised brow, Lauren continued, "For almost a year now, I've worked for myself."

"Ah, I see. What's your specialty?"

"Marketing, promotions, branding and PR. I have a small roster of regular clients and just finished a major campaign for a Southern university. Your mom needed help and I needed…a break…so here I am."

"When was the last time you were in Vegas?"

"Three years ago, for a friend's wedding."

"So you haven't been to our new hotel."

"No," Lauren replied. She looked beyond Christian and out the window. The limo turned into an impressive entrance bordered by marble waterfalls, the word *CANN* bold, shiny and backlit to stand out in the night. "But I've seen pictures. It looks amazing in magazines and now, up close, is even more impressive."

The limo passed the main entrance and continued to a side door. Christian exited and reached back his hand to help her. "It delights me to hear you say that," he murmured as a uniformed employee opened the door and greeted them. "For CANN, our goal for this location is quite simple—to be the most spectacular hotel in the world. We believe it is."

Once inside, Lauren totally agreed. Unlike other hotels boasting casinos on the Strip, the area they entered was elegant, modern and most of all, quiet.

"Where's the casino?" she asked.

"The main casino is two floors down, accessible by a separate entrance," he answered, pulling out his phone to respond to a text. "There's a private one for high rollers on a higher floor. We'll go later, after dinner, if you'd like. It's a whole other world."

Lauren noticed that the employee who'd opened the door still walked behind them, a respectable distance away. As Christian put away his phone, he saw her glance back and looked, too.

"I don't need anything. You can return to your post."

"Are you sure there isn't anything I can do for you, Mr. Breedlove?"

"Absolutely sure."

"I understand it's your birthday, Mr. Breedlove."

He tsked. "Can't keep a secret around here."

"Not with us," the employee responded with a small smile. "Happy birthday, sir."

Christian walked over and shook the employee's hand. "What's your name?"

"Eric, sir."

"How long have you been a part of our security detail?"

"Was just hired a month ago, sir."

"I think our security manager made a very fine choice. Welcome to the team."

"Thank you, sir."

They continued down the hall and past an opening where Lauren glimpsed a vast lobby filled with well-dressed women and expensively suited men. For many reasons, she was glad they'd come through a private entrance. The paparazzi seemed to live for Christian. A splashy spread announcing her whereabouts was the last thing she needed.

A few moments later, they reached an elevator that blended seamlessly with the wall, its doors boasting the same design. She watched him place his thumb on a scanner discreetly located above a chair rail. When the doors opened, Lauren slipped her arm around the one Christian offered and held on, taking in the landscape of neon lights as the elevator ascended to Zest, the Michelin-starred restaurant she'd read about that was housed on the one-hundredth floor.

The doors parted, and the view from the room took Lauren's breath away. Beyond the semiprivate booths and massive crystal chandelier were floor-to-ceiling windows that gave the illusion that there were no walls, that one could walk to the edge of the floor and touch the sky. The atmosphere in the main dining room was fairly quiet, dim and understated. All of that changed when Christian opened the door to the private dining room.

"Happy birthday, Christian!"

"You're the man, Chris!"

Other shouts and cheers filtered through the applause as those who were sitting got to their feet. Lauren looked at Christian, who'd stopped just inside the door, clearly surprised to see the large crowd that filled the room. Two men broke away from the group and approached them. Had she not known about the twins, Lauren may have thought the champagne had kicked in and caused her to see double. They were identical—tall, dark, handsome, sporting the Breedlove dimple in their left cheek and swagger in their stride.

"The dynamic duo," Christian said once they'd reached him.

"Gotcha, old man!"

"We did it, huh?"

"He didn't see it coming."

"Had no idea!"

Lauren stood mesmerized at the twins' rapid-fire de-livery, sometimes finishing each other's sentences without a pause in between. Her eyes shifted back and forth between them, trying to find a way to differentiate between the two. They had the same soft black curls as Christian, but while his were close-cropped, theirs were longer, wilder. Studying them reminded her of a favorite puzzle at the back of one of her popular fashion magazines, where two pictures that looked identical actually weren't. The test was to find the differences. There were usually several. Here, she was just trying to find even one. Then she spotted it. The one on the left wore a tiny diamond stud in his ear. The one on the right didn't. *Bingo!*

"The dyno duo strikes again!" The two men high-fived before executing an intricate handshake. Their joy and excitement was contagious. Christian was clearly enjoying their friendly verbal sparring match. Just being around them made Lauren smile.

"Where are your manners, Chris?" Diamond Stud asked.

"Yeah, Chris. Introduce us to this beautiful lady."

"To do that you two will have to quit talking."

"Whatever."

Said in stereo. *Cute.*

"Lauren, meet my annoying younger brothers Nicholas Jr." He motioned toward the twin who'd last spoken, the one not wearing an earring. "Called Nick to differentiate between him and my father."

"Hello, Nick," Lauren said, with outstretched hand.

"And Noah."

"Hi, Noah." Again, she offered her hand.

"Ah, no, Lauren. Shaking is for business. Hugging is for friends."

Noah pulled Lauren into a bear hug.

Christian placed his hand on Noah's shoulder. "Back off."

Nick laughed. Christian looked over as a few others headed toward them.

"Tyson!"

Tyson, a striking blond with clear brown eyes, bore a mock scowl as he approached. "You going to stand here by the door all night?"

"You're a trip," Christian said. The two men enjoyed a hearty embrace. "I can't believe how well you helped pull this off. You remembered everything, bro."

"I'm good like that." He looked at Lauren, clearly impressed. "Hello, I'm Tyson Ford."

"Lauren Hart—"

"Hey there, birthday boy!"

Lauren found herself being pushed aside by a whirlwind of haughtiness wearing stilettos and cloaked in what smelled like an entire bottle of perfume. The woman threw her arms around Christian. Lauren looked on, more amused than annoyed. But if she read his expression correctly, for Christian the opposite was true. She watched as he deftly removed the brunette's arms from around his neck, just as more and more of his friends came over to greet him. Soon he was swept into a circle of admirers, all clamoring for attention. From the corner of her eye, Lauren saw someone approach.

"Come, dear," Victoria said, slipping her arm through Lauren's and walking toward the head table. "That was Chloe, who grew up with Chris. I've seated you with the family, beside me, so that I can offer a play-by-play on this motley cast of characters. In order to do your job properly, you'll need not only an in-depth grasp of the CANN conglomerate but also the ocean of high society here in Nevada and beyond…"

She paused and watched Chloe glide back to her table. "And the sharks who swim in those waters."

The next hour was a blur of names and faces as during dinner Victoria pointed out the movers and shakers of metropolitan Las Vegas and the few who resided in Breedlove, the unincorporated Nevada town founded by Nicholas and a few others more than twenty years ago. Lauren was introduced to some of them, along with many of Christian's friends from across the country who'd flown in for the occasion. Once the last dessert plate was removed, a few tables were rearranged to make room for a dance floor. A famous DJ from Miami fired up the crowd.

Nick walked over. "Come on, Lauren. Let's dance."

She waved him away. "It's been a long day. I'd rather just relax and watch all of you."

"Okay, but if you change your mind…"

"I'll come find you."

When Lauren got up a few minutes later, she didn't head to the dance floor. She'd seen Victoria and Nicholas heading toward the exit and after getting their attention, made a beeline toward them to catch a ride to her new home. In the past forty-eight hours, her already-chaotic life had been thrown into further disarray, and she needed time to try to process everything and figure out what would come next.

She felt eyes following her as she crossed to the door, saw Chloe whispering to another girl as she neared the Breedloves and fell into step beside them. She could only imagine what Chloe and all the other socialites were wondering about the new girl, and whether or not she, too, was vying to become the missus of tonight's birthday boy. They needn't worry. While they may be in a footrace to catch a husband, Lauren had upended her life to avoid one.

Three

Am I still dreaming?

Last night, Lauren swore that was true. After the driver dropped off Nicholas and Victoria, he'd continued on for about a mile until reaching a cul-de-sac lined with exquisite single-story homes, all different architecturally and uniquely beautiful. Her immediate favorite was the very first one on the corner lot, a Spanish-inspired design of tan stucco and adobe brick with a black gabled roof. Even in her exhaustion she'd admired the wrought iron accents and arches on the windows and doors. When the driver had pulled into that home's driveway and announced it as the guesthouse chosen for her, Lauren's jaw had dropped.

"I'm staying here? Are you sure?"

"Positive," the driver had responded with a knowing smile. "You'll find your luggage in the bedroom. The residence has been stocked with everything one might need for an extended stay, but just in case you need anything else the guesthouse manager's card is on the table in the foyer." He handed her a small envelope. "Here's the code for the lock. Can you make it in okay?"

"I'm fine."

"Just checking. You look pretty wiped out."

She had been, but from exhaustion, not from too much drinking as she believed the driver assumed. It had taken her a couple tries to key in the correct code, but upon opening the door, it was like entering the abode of a fairy tale. The decor was straight out of *Architectural Digest*.

And now, awakening on the cloudlike memory foam bed after a blissful night's sleep, the dream had yet to dissipate. She sighed contentedly. The sun was shining. She was well rested. And everything that had happened, all that she'd seen, was real.

Lauren sat up, stretched and reached for her phone. She tapped the face. "Oh my God!" It was after 10:00 a.m. An early riser since college, Lauren couldn't recall the last time she'd slept this late, even after a night of partying. She'd even slept through the telephone ringing, with missed calls from Avery, her bestie, and her mom, Faye. Victoria had told her to come by after she'd risen for a casual visit. Lauren had said to expect her around nine o'clock. Now she'd be lucky to get there by eleven.

After sending Victoria a quick text requesting they meet at eleven, she took a quick shower, pulled her hair into a high ponytail, and hurriedly donned a free-flowing, light yellow maxi dress, silver jewelry that included her ever-present charm bracelet and a pair of ivory-colored sandals with cute yet comfy wedge heels. She arrived at the front door of what could only be described as a mansion with two minutes to spare.

A middle-aged Hispanic woman with coal-black hair and kind eyes opened the door.

"Hello, are you Lauren?"

"Yes."

"The missus is expecting you. Please, come this way."

Lauren entered a wide foyer with art-lined textured walls and slate tile, with hues of orange, tan, blue and ivory, colors that were repeated throughout the home's elegant yet comfortable decor. One hallway flowed into another. To the right was a formal dining room with huge single-paned windows that not only let in loads of natural sunlight but showcased the beautiful and meticulously landscaped garden in the expansive backyard. They turned left down a short hall that ended at ornately crafted French doors, standing ajar. Beyond that was a great room with two-story ceilings, chandeliers and one wall that seemed made entirely of glass.

Victoria was seated on an oversize tan sectional boasting soft Italian leather. She was wearing a short floral caftan and crystal-covered sandals. Seeing her in the bright, natural light of day made her even more beautiful than when Lauren first hugged her last night. Her pixie hairstyle framed a face devoid of wrinkles, one that looked more like thirtysomething than what Lauren knew was actually fifty-plus years. She turned and smiled when Lauren entered, put down the magazine she'd been reading and patted the space beside her.

"Well, good morning, sunshine!"

"Good morning, Victoria."

Lauren sat, then leaned over to accept the older woman's embrace.

"Look at you, all fresh-faced and fabulous. You woke up like that?"

Lauren laughed. "Not quite."

"But you're not wearing makeup."

"No. I hope that's okay. You said this would be a casual meeting, so…"

"Oh, no. It's fine. I'm just impressed. Not many women in my circle would be caught dead without their war paint."

"I do have on mascara," Lauren admitted. "And lip gloss."

"That's all? Must be nice."

"I could say the same about you. You look more like Christian's sister than his mom."

"Not without effort. Our hotel spa has some of the best aestheticians in the country, who are always researching the latest skin-tightening, wrinkle-eliminating, turn-back-the-time trends." Victoria placed a hand on Lauren's arm. "I was just about to have a light lunch. Care to join me?"

"Sure, thanks."

Victoria turned toward the woman who'd opened the front door, standing so quietly Lauren hadn't realized she was still there. "Sofia, tell Gabe we'll have the quinoa and spinach salad with sparkling cranberry orange juice. Thank you."

Victoria watched Sofia nod and leave the room. Her eyes shifted to Lauren. "Did you rest well?"

"The best sleep ever. I barely remember my head hitting the pillow."

"You'd had a busy two days."

"Yes."

"And…somewhat of a tumultuous time before that." Lauren nodded. "Faye didn't go into detail and you need only share what you'd like, but when I mentioned my assistant's abrupt departure and that I needed to replace her ASAP, she all but accepted the job for you. Said time away from the East Coast was exactly what you needed right now."

"She was right." Lauren took a deep breath, on one hand nervous to share the personal dilemma while on the other compelled to confide in someone with an unbiased point of view. "What exactly did Mom tell you?"

"That you were in a difficult relationship, one exacerbated by the fact that he's the son of your dad's employer?"

Lauren's chuckle held no humor. "That's one way to say it." She looked Victoria in the eye. "My dad is trying to force me into a marriage that would be bad on the home front but apparently good for business."

"Force as in…like an arranged marriage?"

"Yes."

"Well, that's just ridiculous. This is the twenty-first century, and while I've known more than one desperate soul who's walked down the aisle for money, I'd counsel any woman who asked to marry for love."

Lauren watched myriad expressions flit across Victoria's face as she processed the situation.

"What does Faye say about it?"

"Basically, she agrees with you, and so do I. But Dad is really pushing the idea, almost desperately so. Being married to the man orchestrating the idea puts her in a difficult position. She wants what's best for both of us, but he can be very persuasive."

"You say this guy's father is your dad's boss?"

Lauren nodded. "Years ago, when Dad sought investors for his accounting firm, Gerald was first in line with an open checkbook. The future looked promising, but in the end, Dad's small company couldn't compete with the intellectual diversity and electronic wizardry of the larger firms."

She released a breath, then continued.

"While Dad had struggled, Gerald's consulting firm had grown by leaps and bounds. When his CFO took an early retirement, he called my dad, who felt he owed it to Gerald, given the investment he'd made and never gotten back."

"Gerald sounds like a good friend. But if your dad is already in an executive position, how would you marrying the son make business better?"

"I don't know." Lauren paused, wondering just how much she should tell Victoria. "Can I trust what we discuss to remain just between us?"

"Absolutely, Lauren."

"Shared with no one, not even my mom?"

Victoria placed a hand on Lauren's arm and squeezed. "Not even Faye, darling."

"Years ago, Ed and I briefly dated."

"The son."

"Yes. I was a freshman in college. He's eight years older than me. I was young, dumb, impressionable and thrilled to get the attention of an older, successful man. Mere weeks into dating, he gave me a ring. A promise ring that we both assumed would lead to an engagement. But it didn't."

"Why not?"

"Because in time I realized that Ed's well-put-together image was a facade hiding a controlling narcissist who was verbally abusive. I gave back the ring and ended the relationship. I don't think he ever got over it. Ed's an only child used to getting what he wants."

"Your parents didn't know?"

"They knew we'd dated but not why we broke up. I never told them about anything—the verbal and emotional abuse, his anger issues, definitely not about the ring. Our parents are friends and I didn't want to cause trouble between them. Anyway, a while back, I heard that he'd been boasting about an upcoming engagement to a young, naive but really pretty girl. Something happened and the relationship abruptly ended. And then…"

Victoria raised a brow but remained silent.

"He tried to get me back, tried to force me into a relationship by reminding me of the promise I'd made and admitting his fault in our not working out. When I rebuffed his overtures, things got ugly."

"How so?"

"He demanded that I marry him, and if I didn't comply, he threatened to make things difficult for my family. Of course I told him hell would freeze over before I got involved with him again." She released a quavering breath. "I don't know what he told my dad, but now two men are trying to force my hand."

"Did you ask Paul why?"

"Yes, and Dad's answers don't make sense, nor does the chummy friendship that seems to exist between them. In the past few months they've really ramped up the pressure. This break is a godsend, so thanks again."

The women paused as Sofia returned bearing a tray of warm homemade rolls, a pitcher of juice and a crystal bowl filled with the spinach and quinoa salad that Victoria had requested. When conversation resumed, the topic shifted from Lauren's personal life to the freelance marketing work she'd handled over the past twelve months and the professional duties she'd take on as Victoria's personal assistant, work that would largely center on the CANN Foundation.

"I'm sorry to overwhelm you," Victoria finished. "But next week's tea and fashion show has become a hugely popular event. That this one takes place around Valentine's Day, focuses on love and features some hunky eye candy along with the fashion has made it even bigger. But between the two of us, I think we'll be fine."

"I do, too," Lauren said, zipping up her tablet cover and placing the computer inside her tote. "It's a lot of work, for sure, but I love being busy and I'm a huge fan of Ace Montgomery, his wife London and the HER Fashion line. I'll do everything in my power to ensure the event goes off without a hitch."

"There's one last thing, Lauren." Victoria reached for a folder on the table before her. "I've drawn up a six-month contract covering from now until July 15. Had I had one before I wouldn't have been left high and dry without help. I hope you don't mind signing it."

"On the contrary, I'd be delighted. That means it's literally illegal for me to return home."

Small talk continued as Victoria walked Lauren to the door, with Lauren commenting on the original art pieces that lined the hallway. They stepped outside to a clear, cloudless sky and a subtle warm breeze. "Where's the car?" she asked.

Along with the guesthouse, a car had been placed at Lauren's disposal. She had yet to drive it.

"I walked here," Lauren replied. "The dry air is a wonderful change from Maryland's humidity, and weather this warm in February rarely happens back east. Plus I haven't worked out lately, and can use the exercise."

"Just so you're sure, because I'd be more than happy to have someone drive you home."

"No, thanks, I'll be fine."

The women hugged. Lauren waved and headed down the circular drive to the sidewalk that cut through an expansive lawn, toward the paved road. The two-mile-long walk was barely remembered, so consumed was she with the amount of work she'd need to handle to help Victoria pull off next week's fashion show. She'd wanted to escape Ed, the pressure from her father and a predictable life, but as she reached the front door of her lovely Spanish-styled home, Lauren couldn't help but ask herself, had she jumped from the frying pan into the fryer?

Lauren entered the home and headed toward the dining room table, pulling the tablet from her tote while crossing the room. She wanted to go over the notes while the conversation with Victoria was still fresh in her mind. Tossing her tote on the couch, she pulled a bottle of water from the fridge, then sat and fired up the tablet. That's when she noticed something missing—her charm bracelet.

A pang of fear seized Lauren's chest as she jumped up from the chair, retrieved the tote and began searching inside it. The bracelet had been her talisman since receiving it as a birthday gift at the age of sixteen. She'd moved cross-country to dodge domineering men and take control of her future. Now would be the worst possible time for her luck to run out.

With no success from a search inside, Lauren reached for the sandals she'd kicked off upon entering the house. She slipped them on and opened the front door. Just before stepping outside, her cell phone rang. *Victoria, maybe?* Had she found the bracelet on the manse's exquisite marble floors? Lauren hoped so, and hurried to catch the call before it went to voice mail.

"Lauren Hart." Her greeting came out in a rush of panicked air.

"I know who I called," a familiar voice answered.

"Oh, Avery. Hi." Lauren headed back toward the still-open front door.

"Obviously not who you were expecting," Avery

said. "Which answers my second question after 'How are you?' which is 'Have you seen your teen crush?' Is that who you thought was calling?"

"Actually, I was hoping it was Victoria, his mom."

"Oh."

"I lost my bracelet and was hoping she'd found it."

"Your good luck charms? Oh, no!"

"Exactly. I'm trying not to freak out."

"Don't do that. Just think of all the places you've been and retrace your steps."

"That's what I'm getting ready to do." Lauren stepped back inside the home and headed toward her closet for a more comfortable pair of shoes.

"Can I call you back?"

"Not before an update, a short version at least, since my phone calls have not been returned."

Lauren retrieved her tennis shoes, sat on the bed and put the call on speaker. "From the second I touched down, it's been a whirlwind. I was going to call you tonight."

"So you had to start work as soon as you landed?"

"No, but in some ways that's how it felt, and that's after being in transit for almost eight hours."

"Why did you book a flight with that many changes, or such a long layover?"

"To be a part of Christian's birthday surprise. Yesterday was his thirtieth birthday. His parents surprised him with a slew of gifts and I was a part of that package."

"What?" The single syllable held out for several seconds suggested there were many more questions behind it.

Lauren laughed. "Not like that! His parents bought him a private plane and wanted me to fly in on it. So I took a flight to Atlanta, where the Gulfstream was

adoring eyes who'd watched him when she thought he wasn't looking. The kid he'd brushed off or ignored while pursuing her older sister.

What it was about Lauren that now had him so enthralled Christian didn't know, except that it was something that none of the other women he'd been around lately possessed. It wasn't just her beauty, though she was gorgeous, with features she seemed to have been born with rather than purchased. Christian had been around and dated some of the most beautiful women on the planet. What attracted him to Lauren was a mystery, one he was determined to solve.

Christian pulled into the driveway, cutting off the engine and stepping out in one smooth motion. Ignoring his increased heartbeat, he strolled to the front door and rang the bell. Several long moments passed and he lifted his hand to knock just as the door opened.

"Oh. It's you."

Christian took in Lauren's bouncy ponytail and colorful sneakers, and the way her darkly bronzed skin glimmered against the pale yellow dress draped so becomingly over her curves. She looked absolutely delectable, and he prided himself on resisting the urge to lick his lips or kiss hers.

"Who were you expecting?"

"Um, someone else."

She seemed distracted, swiping an errant strand of hair away from her face as she looked at the floor around her.

"Am I interrupting?"

"Actually, I was just heading out to look for something."

"This, maybe?" He held up a silver link bracelet with dangling charms.

"Yes!" She reached for the bracelet.

Christian pulled back.

"Chris, give it to me. Now."

"Only if you'll be kind enough to invite me inside." He meant that in all ways imaginable.

"Sure," she said, stepping back.

He moved inside, stopped directly in front of her, just a few inches and a wall of heat between them.

"Now give me the bracelet."

"Ask nicely."

"May I have the bracelet, please?" Said through gritted teeth with flashing eyes.

Christian laughed. He unclasped the bracelet. "Here, allow me."

"Where did you find it?"

"At the edge of the circular drive. I saw it just before going up the steps."

She eyed him suspiciously. "Come on now," he drawled, then grinned. "It's why I came over, to give it back."

"Really? I can't tell." She held out her arm and smiled as he placed the delicate silver chain around her slender wrist and looked into her eyes. She returned his stare— bold, unflinching. Obviously the shy, awkward tween was all grown up. He hooked the clasp, then, still holding her arm with one hand, turned the bracelet with the other and reached for one of several charms, this one a heart.

"Each of these has a meaning, right?"

"Yes."

Christian's thumb brushed the inside of her wrist. An unasked question was immediately answered as Lauren's nipples hardened and pressed against soft cotton. She wore no bra. Acutely aware of his gaze, Lauren eased her wrist from his grasp and crossed her arms over her chest.

He observed the move but made no comment. Was she

sincerely embarrassed? Playing hard to get? *What does it matter to you?* It didn't, Christian reminded himself. He'd had enough experience with women to know that even if she agreed to a casual affair, emotions could shift and life could get ugly. She could become a stalker or worse, somehow try to trap him. He knew that when it came to temporary liaisons, it was best to keep a safe distance between his lovers and his family and professional life. That wouldn't be the case with Lauren. Their mothers were very good friends. Even more, Lauren was now his mother's assistant. Which meant she was off-limits.

Life wasn't fair.

"A heart, huh?"

"Yep." Lauren fingered the silver trinket, her eyes on him as her headlights dimmed. She'd gotten her body under control, he saw, at least for the moment.

"So since you're wearing it on your sleeve, so to speak, does that mean no one has it yet?"

"That was really bad, Christian." She turned and walked into the living room, toward the couch. "Like something you would have asked my sister when you were sixteen."

"Yeah, it was pretty lame." He pointed to the couch. "May I?"

"Of course. I'm sorry, where are my manners? Would you like something to drink?"

"No, I'm fine."

Lauren joined him on the brushed-suede sofa. He moved to lessen the distance between them. As one hand encircled her wrist, the other fingered another charm on the bracelet. "Does this signify your wild side?"

"If so, I'd be quite dangerous. Bears are strong. That's the mascot of my alma mater's football team."

"Which is…?"

"Morgan State."

"I see."

"Are you into college sports?"

"Not too much, and not football. My games are golf, basketball and tennis. A little pro baseball every now and then. Are you a big sports fan?"

"I like football."

"So if I decided to tackle you, it would be all right?"

"You could try, but I might rise up on hind legs and swipe you with my paw." Christian chuckled as Lauren continued. "Leave a trail of fingernail scratches across your body. But then again, that probably wouldn't be the first time."

"Except for my brothers or teammates, being attacked would absolutely be a first. I'm not a violent man."

"What about the women you date, like Chloe?"

"What makes you think I dated her? Mom told you?"

"You and your life were not a part of our conversation. Chloe's reaction toward me said it all. If evil eyes were daggers, I wouldn't have lasted the night."

"Chloe doesn't like to be outshone, and you were the brightest star in the room," he murmured. "We've known each other for years, basically grew up together, and dated off and on in high school. What about you? What does your boyfriend think about you moving cross-country to take a job?"

"Is that your roundabout way of asking whether or not there's a man in my life?"

"Is there?" he asked.

"No."

Christian quirked a brow. "That doesn't seem possible."

"Perhaps, but it's true. My last serious relationship

was a while ago. After that I threw myself into work, networking and building up my client base."

"And you left all you'd built to work with my mom?" he probed.

"Victoria knows I have ongoing clients and believes I can handle the work required for them and help her out, too."

Christian studied Lauren as she talked, knowing she held back much more than she'd spoken. She hardly seemed the all-work-and-no-play sort of woman. Patience was one of the traits that made Christian such an astute businessman. Patience and intuition, knowing when to hold and when to fold. So he held his curiosity for why she'd leave a growing clientele to work for a nonprofit foundation with his mother. But still, he wondered. Was she running away from something? Was she part of his mother's plan to turn him into a married man? Did she have plans of her own?

"How old are you?"

"Twenty-six. I'll be twenty-seven in April."

"You called me an old man last night but you're not too far from thirty yourself."

"Getting older is not the worst thing that can happen, you know."

"But it seems to be harder for women than for men. Don't you want to get married and raise a family?"

Christian had asked the questions casually, but he listened intently as she answered.

"At some point that might be nice, if I find the right man. Why?" She looked at him from beneath long, curly lashes, her smile reigniting the desire that had sprung up when she opened the door. "Are you applying for the job?"

"I already have a wife." He laughed as shock registered in her eyes. "Her name is CANN."

"Then—" Lauren leaned toward him "—a mistress, maybe?"

"Careful, beautiful lady. You're about to start a fire."

"You're right. I shouldn't tease."

"No, you shouldn't. Don't poke the bear."

Five

Lauren said she was teasing, but she wasn't. She *wanted* to poke the bear and stroke the undeniable heat between them into a massive flame, and then spend a night or twelve putting it out. All the while knowing the very last thing she needed was a meaningless fling, a too-close-for-comfort friend with benefits.

But she'd been guarded for a very long time. And Christian was so damn sexy. Being in close proximity to him had caused the embers from her childhood crush to catch a spark. His smoldering gaze and gentle touch on the pulse of her wrist had turned that spark into crackling flames. Lauren's body was on fire, and the man who owned the hose that could put it out was sitting right beside her.

She watched Christian deftly adjust his pants as he shifted his body away from her. It was good to know she wasn't the only one being physically affected in this moment. He checked his watch. The movement brought her attention to his long, masculine fingers and neatly manicured nails. Imagining the goose bumps that would arise if he ran them lightly across her body, she reached for his hand for a closer examination. He pulled it away.

"Really, Christian? If I didn't know better I'd say there was a hint of fear in your eyes. Are you afraid that I might be too much to handle?"

"I can't remember the last time I've been afraid of anything," Christian answered, a comment that sounded arrogant except Lauren had a feeling it was probably true. "There's definitely never been a woman to make me show fear."

"Then what was that? You aren't in a relationship. You admit you find me attractive. You say you like sex. Wait. Are you experiencing erectile dysfunction?" They both laughed. "Do we need to get you a little blue pill?"

Christian chuckled. "There are no physical problems when it comes to my ability to function sexually. I am the epitome of a virile male."

"Is that so?" He nodded. "Prove it."

Christian's gaze changed, intensified. His irises darkened, dropped to her lips. She licked them, waited, watched the muscles in his arm ripple with tension, like a feral black panther ready to pounce. But he didn't. He stood and reached for her hand.

"Walk me to the door, pretty lady."

Lauren steeled herself. She already knew that electricity flowed when their skin touched, so she braced herself for the shock. What she wasn't prepared for, however, was that after standing she'd be pulled into Christian's arms and seared with a kiss that made her gasp. Or that he'd take that opportunity to deepen the exchange. Skilled and demanding, his tongue was like a sword in the hands of a master—cutting away at her defenses, carving a place for himself in her world.

Lauren wanted more and took a step closer. She slid her hands up and over strong, broad shoulders, heard him groan and felt his hand moving toward her butt. When her hand began a similar journey, she felt him stiffen beneath her touch. He stepped back. The apology forming on her lips was interrupted by his ringing cell phone.

"Still popular, I see."

"Comes with the territory," he said with a shrug. He straightened to a height at least six inches taller than her five-foot-eight frame, tweaked her nose. "Are you coming to the house tomorrow?"

"I don't know. The past few days have been a whirlwind and my job officially starts on Monday, so… I might take the time to get settled, maybe check out the town a bit."

"All right, then. Go easy on these Vegas cowboys. Somebody like you will be hard for them to handle."

"Thanks for the advice, partna," Lauren drawled.

Christian laughed as he opened the door and stepped out. His dimple offered a flirty wink while his taut butt and long, muscular legs gave a final adios. And what a goodbye stroll!

Lauren closed the door and leaned against it. She took a deep breath to calm the flutters in her stomach…and elsewhere. Amazing how unwanted events completely out of her control had landed her in Nevada, the Wild West, in very close proximity to the first man she'd ever desired.

Christian had no need to worry about any other of the town's broncos. He was the only stallion she wanted to ride.

The next morning Lauren's cell phone rang at six o'clock, but it didn't wake her. A restless night had given way to morning. Thoughts of Christian warred with the nightmare of a situation that her dad had created. Bad business choices, the partnership he desired. And the piece of the puzzle she hadn't shared with Victoria—his ultimatum about marrying Ed. When she picked up her cell phone and saw her mom's picture, Lauren felt unexpected tears threatening to erupt. She forced down the emotion and took a breath before sitting up and hitting the speaker button.

"Good morning, Mom."

"It's morning but there's very little that's good about it."

"Why? What's the matter?" she asked anxiously.

"Your dad was under the impression that you were on a weekend getaway. He's furious to learn that you'll be gone for months."

"Which is why I asked you to let me handle telling him."

"I know, but when he asked what time you'd be returning today, I couldn't lie."

"I'm sorry for putting you in the middle of this. But when it comes to marrying Ed, Dad's encouragement has turned to insistence." She sighed. "Telling him about taking the job with Victoria would have made it much harder to leave. Besides, I told you that I would call him later and explain everything."

"I know, but we've been married for more than three decades. He knew something was going on."

"What did you tell him?" Lauren demanded.

"That you were working with Vickie and—"

"Mom! You told him I was here, in Vegas? The next thing you know he'll be showing up on the Strip!"

Or even worse, Ed will.

"Better that I told him rather than he find out on his

own," her mother reminded her. "Now everything's aboveboard and it doesn't look like you're running away."

She huffed out a breath. "But that's exactly what I'm doing!"

"You can't run forever, Lauren."

"I can't marry Ed, either, and I'm sick of being pressured about it."

Her mother released an audible sigh. "Hopefully whatever business deal he and Ed are working on can proceed without you being in the middle."

"Business deal? What are you talking about?"

Faye's voice lowered. "We'll talk more later. I've got to go. Call your father."

Her mother's calling had roused Lauren from sleep, but any chance of reclaiming her snooze fled with Faye's unintended announcement. *What kind of deal could Ed have that would involve Dad?*

Lauren rolled out of bed. After a quick turn in the bathroom, she pulled on a pair of baggy shorts, a white tee over a striped sports bra, and a pair of tennis shoes. After placing a pair of earbuds into her cell phone's jack, she slipped the phone into an armband, grabbed an apple from the bowl of fruit on her bar counter and headed out the door.

The sun had risen but the sky was hazy, providing a cool breeze for the beginning of her run. She looked in the direction of the mansion and pointedly ran the opposite way. With what her mother had shared fresh in her mind, she wanted to avoid seeing any of the Breedloves—especially Christian.

Mortification swept through her. What had she been *thinking* yesterday coming on to him like that? Their families had known each other for years, but what did that matter? They'd known the Millers a long time too.

She'd thought she knew Ed. He was good-looking, with a brooding disposition that she'd at first considered sexy but now knew hid a jerky personality. Who was to say that Christian wasn't an ass, too? That a phone call had interrupted her attempt at seduction was probably the best thing that could have happened. It might have helped her dodge a bullet headed straight for her heart.

Lauren stilled her mind and focused on running, her steps rhythmic, measured, her breath paced as evenly as her steps. The surroundings were beautiful, vast stretches of green grass that had to have been specially planted, a stark contrast to the browns, blues and grays of the mountain range and brightening sky. She followed the road, kept time with the beat and let herself get lost in the rhythm of the world around her. Time fell away. So did her problems, as she chose not to focus on the conversation with her mom, or why she'd left Maryland.

She took in the mountains and the pines and…*cows*? Lauren slowed her pace. The farther she went the more cows she saw. Dozens? Hundreds? And then she saw him. A ranch hand? A cowboy? Indeed, and galloping straight toward her.

Lauren slowed to a walk, then stopped and watched the rider approach, noting the darkly tanned forearms tightly holding the reins. *Christian?* Certain body muscles clenched at the mere possibility. So she changed focus and looked at the horse instead. A Thoroughbred from the looks of it, black and majestic. Like Christian. It had been years since she'd gone riding, but her love of horses came back with the magnificent creature's every stride.

Rider and horse reached a fence that was jumped and cleared by at least two feet. He pulled on the reins and the Thoroughbred slowed. Finally, the rider took off a worn cowboy hat.

"Good morning, gorgeous."

"Adam, good morning! I wondered who was hiding under the hat."

"I see you're an early riser. A runner, too."

"Guilty on both counts," she confessed. "That's a beautiful horse."

"Do you ride?"

"It's been a while."

"Would you like to? You'll want to change into jeans or long pants first, then I can put you on a filly. They're tamer than the stallions all day long."

"So it's a stallion, huh?" Lauren took cautious steps forward, her tone soothing as the horse watched her with apprehensive eyes. "What's his name?"

"Thunder."

"Of course. It suits him. Hello, Thunder." She slowly moved her hand toward his mane. He bobbed his head but didn't back away. "There you go, beautiful fella. No need to be afraid."

Lauren continued talking, her tone soothing. She remembered the apple in her pocket and pulled it out. She looked at Adam. "May I?"

"No, thanks, I've had breakfast."

Laughter burst forth at the unexpected comment. "Not you, silly, the horse."

"Oh, sure."

She noted Adam's eyes had the same twinkle as Christian's. One thing about those Breedlove men, they were a roguishly handsome bunch.

Lauren waved the apple under Thunder's nose. "Would you like a bite?"

Thunder nodded, opened his mouth and took the apple from her.

"Okay, you've paid the price of entry and made a friend. Ready to ride?"

"Sure, why not? I am in the Wild West, after all."

"Here, take my hand."

Lauren mounted the horse in one smooth motion and settled in behind Adam. As he steered the horse toward the guesthouse where she could change clothes, his phone rang.

"Chris!"

A familiar voice came through Adam's cell phone speakers. "What's up, bro?"

He guided Thunder into a soft trot. "Out riding, like I do most mornings. What are you doing?"

Lauren held on to Adam's shoulders. Hearing Christian's voice increased her heartbeat. If she was unable to quell these physical reactions at the mere sound of his voice, she decided, then working for Victoria was going to be challenge.

"Golf? Right now? Sounds boring, buddy. I'm heading to the mountains, going to show Lauren the view from Breedlove Peak. Yeah, she's with me now." He paused for a moment. "She was out running so I invited her for a ride. Listen, let me holler at you later. We're headed to Lauren's house so she can change clothes and then to the stables to get her saddled up. Thunder is getting restless and wants to run. All right, cool. Talk to you later."

"That was Chris," Adam said as Thunder ate up the distance with his smooth, increased gait. "He said to tell you hello."

"I couldn't help overhearing that it was him on the phone," she replied, raising her voice to be heard above the horse's clomping and the wind. "I heard his voice but not the entire conversation. He's on his way to play golf?"

"No, he's headed to my house."

"How do you figure? I heard what he said."

"Because I told him you were with me. So, trust me, he's on his way."

Six

"Helen," Christian called out to the house manager who'd been employed by the family for almost twenty years. He felt just as he had years ago as a teenager, when he'd been caught sneaking into the house past curfew. More than once Helen had been a lifesaver, fussing at him for disobeying his parents while warning that she'd keep his secret of coming in late only if he maintained a grade point average of 4.0. Christian graduated at the top of his class.

Helen turned around, her face scrunched as she squinted to see who'd called her. "Chris? Goodness gracious, boy, what are you doing coming in over here?"

"Because I knew it was where you'd be." He flashed a charming smile and wrapped his arms around the diminutive woman, lifting her off the floor.

"You're so full of it, and too grown to be sneaking into the opposite wing. What are you after?"

"I could never fool you. My riding boots. I think the last time I used them I left them here."

Helen smiled, her eyes twinkling with mischief. "What, no golf today? That's how you usually spend Sunday morning."

"Thought I'd try something different," was Christian's casual reply.

"Wouldn't have anything to do with the pretty girl Adam took out on the range now, would it?"

"Absolutely not!" He hoped he looked appropriately insulted.

It cracked Helen up, and she swatted at his broad shoulder and barely missed. "You forget that I've known you since you were a kid."

"You're right, Helen. Hard to get anything past you."

"Even harder to try to slip past your mother." The housekeeper crossed the hallway, reached just inside the door of a room on the opposite side and pulled out a pair of worn black leather cowboy boots. "After talking with Adam, she thought you might be motivated to take a ride and had me retrieve them from your old bedroom."

Christian feigned annoyance and snatched the boots from Helen's hands. "Be careful!" she called out behind his retreating back.

"Love you, Helen!"

Christian hopped in the SUV he used to tool around the grounds. He couldn't help grinning at the whole situation, even though he was also chagrined. Helen was right. There was no getting around Victoria's motherly intuition. He'd rarely been able to keep something totally hidden from her. The saying that moms had eyes in the backs of their heads? From the time he was a kid, Christian knew this to be true.

A few twists and turns later, opposite the parcel of

land that housed his five-thousand-square-foot bachelor pad, Christian drove through the iron-and-brick gate
announcing one's entry into Breedlove Beef, the award-
winning business that Adam and his partners had built
from scratch and made profitable in four short years.
He continued down the road, past Adam's innovatively
designed ranch house with interlocking pavilions that
seamlessly combined indoor and outdoor living, traveling along the ruggedly landscaped terrain to the horse
stables behind the barn.

Turning off the engine, he reached for the cowboy
boots he'd retrieved from the house, smiling at the weath-
ered face coming to greet him.

"Well, I'll be damned!" was the gruffly voiced greeting from a man whose taut, wiry frame belied over six
decades of hard cowboy living. "What brings you down
from the crystal tower to wallow in the mud with the
rest of us?"

"Shut up, old man," Christian said, pulling the grand-
fatherly figure everyone called Rusty into a hearty embrace.

"Wait a minute, I know. It's that fine filly I just saddled up. The one whose bass drum is full and plump and
made to both sit in a saddle and ride at the same time."

"Lauren's a lady, Rusty. Show some respect." Christian shook his head, still smiling. "You haven't changed
a bit."

"Too old to change." Rusty pointed out a bench just
inside the stable. "Sit there and pull your boots on. You
need chaps, too?"

"I'm going for a ride, not a roundup."

"Shit," Rusty answered, holding out the word far longer than four letters required. "Tell that to somebody who
hasn't known you since you were knee-high to a gnat.

You're about to round up that sweet darling who trotted out of here on the back of Old Glory."

"You put Lauren on that old nag?"

"That old nag, as you put it, can hold her own against any young filly any day of the week. Push come to shove and a situation needed escaping, I'd put my money on OG."

Rusty disappeared inside the stable. Christian pulled on the well-worn boots and then strode over to a wall of saddles and pulled down a lightweight, dark brown leather one embellished with silver tacks, conchos and corner plates. He reached into a wooden box and after feeling a few, decided on a brightly colored Navajo blanket over the more expensive pads. The sound of softly clopping hooves caused him to turn. He came face-to-face with a young palomino standing regal and strong, eyeing him intently.

Christian's tone was gentle, soothing as he made proper acquaintance, patting the horse's coat before saddling up and mounting the frisky steed. Christian immediately tightened the reins, gently pressing a heel into the horse's side to direct him and establish control. The palomino dipped his head in agreement, as if to say "you're the boss."

"Good boy, Biscuit. You and I will do just fine."

"That's a load of power you've got there," Rusty said. "You sure you don't need me to take you on a turn or two inside the corral before you ride him across the prairie?"

"Thanks, but I've got this." Christian steered the horse toward the stable exit, as comfortable in the saddle as in a boardroom chair. "Which way did they go?"

"Ah, so you *are* on a roundup."

"Rusty…"

"Toward the mountain," the old man answered, amid

the enjoyment of a good guffaw. "She's worth riding for, my boy. Go get her."

Christian intended to do just that, and with the wide-open landscape, Lauren and his brother weren't hard to find. He spotted them on the winding trail leading to Breedlove Peak, where the boys had spent countless hours as children, target shooting, catching prey and roughhousing.

With his goal in sight, Christian allowed the palomino to run freely, quickly closing the gap between them. Adam was the first to see him approach. Christian watched as his brother led his horse closer to the one Lauren rode. Seconds later, she turned and waved. Christian ignored the tightening in his groin as he led the horse toward the mountain trail.

"Look who's up before noon," Adam said as Christian approached. "You really are getting older, big brother. I would have thought you'd have partied the whole weekend."

Christian pulled up alongside Adam. The two enjoyed a hearty handshake. "Ty and the rest of the guys are on their way to the airport. Felt a bit of fresh air would do the body good." He looked over at Lauren, his eyes quickly scanning her from head to toe. Rusty was right. She sat the hell out of that saddle. Again, his groin tightened, this time making it harder to ignore. He shifted in the saddle in order to covertly adjust himself.

"Good morning, beautiful."

"Good morning, Chris."

Damn if those eyes and sultry voice didn't make him want to lift the blanket from his horse's back, throw it on the ground and lay her on top of it. Just the thought of her here, in the sunlight, naked and wanton, required him to make another adjustment. He needed to do something quick, before he embarrassed them all.

"Hey, brother. Is the cave still there?"

Adam nodded. "Of course."

"Cave?" Lauren asked curiously.

"Depending on the day," Christian explained, "as kids it was everything from a science lab to Matrix headquarters to our hideout after getting in trouble with Dad. Want to see it?"

"I'm game for whatever," she replied.

Christian's eyes darkened as he digested her words. "I'll keep that in mind."

The trio continued to a plateau near the top of the mountain. They dismounted their horses and continued over rocks and small bushes to a side of the mountain away from the sun.

"Do you remember where it is?" Christian asked.

Adam looked over his shoulder at him, smirked and kept walking. He reached a crevice in what appeared to be a large boulder.

"Do you see it?"

"Here, let me help you." Christian reached for Lauren's hand as he walked toward Adam. "See what?"

He stepped to the rock, ran his hand along a narrow seam. His eyes sparkled like the ten-year-old he was when they'd discovered it. "The triple *S*."

"The secret silver sliver. Yes, indeed."

The two brothers grabbed a large slab of rock and watched Lauren's expression go from skepticism to amazement as the cave entrance came into view and Christian pulled her inside.

"Stay close to me," he whispered, sliding a hand around her waist and coming precariously close to her delectable backside. "The bogeyman might get you in the dark."

"Are you the bogeyman?" Lauren retorted, gripping

his waist to keep her balance over a dirt floor strewn with potholes and rocks.

Glad for the opportunity her unsteadiness presented, Christian slid his arm around her and pulled her closer. "Woman, haven't I warned you? You're about to get in all kinds of trouble."

"Promises, promises," she cooed.

"I can't believe they're still here…" Adam said into the darkness before setting fire to a huge glob of wax that at one time had been a group of individual candles now melted into a ghostlike creation. Soon the space was illuminated enough for Christian to make out Lauren's luscious lips. The flickering candle brought them in and out of focus. He felt her hand fall away from his body as a web of undeniable desire began to wrap itself around them until he and Lauren were the only ones there. Her lips, her body, the heat drew him closer…

"…since the last time we were here. That was what, Chris, about ten years ago?"

The sound of Adam's voice penetrated the fog of need, lust and almost primitive hunger stirring in Christian's gut.

"Um, yeah, even further back than that. I think my last time spending the night here was when I was fifteen, sixteen years old."

Sixteen…the last time he'd seen Lauren until two days ago. When his testosterone was in overdrive and she was still a kid. That was then. This was now. Lauren had grown into a sexy-ass woman who clearly knew how to go after what she wanted, and she'd made it clear that what she wanted was him. The feeling was mutual and in this moment, while he knew that he shouldn't cross that line, the truth of the matter was he couldn't help himself.

He wanted to taste more of what Lauren so freely offered, wanted to give his body to her so she could ride him all night long. It was time to cut short the trip down memory lane and land squarely back in the present. Fortunately, Adam was thinking the exact same thing.

"All right, guys, enough time in the dungeon." He blew out the candles. "Let's get out of here."

They walked outside and though they'd only been in the cave a few minutes, the weather had warmed under a sun-drenched sky. The trio headed to the horses and untied the reins that had been looped over a well-worn iron hitching post on the plateau embedded in stone.

Adam placed a foot in the stirrup and swung up in a graceful motion. "Ready to head to the top of the mountain?"

She shook her head. "No, it's getting hot. I think I'll head back down."

"I thought you liked the heat," Christian murmured. The way Lauren's eyes swept over his body proved she'd gotten the double entendre.

Adam had finally gotten the hint, too. A wagon of romance was starting to roll, and he was the third wheel. "On that note, big brother, it appears that my job is done. I'll see you guys at brunch." He turned Thunder and guided the horse past Christian, stopping to let Lauren turn Old Glory around. "You follow me and let Christian bring up the rear," he instructed. "When it comes to us and horseback riding, coming in last is familiar territory for him.

"See you at the stables." With that, a sure-footed Thunder headed down the sloping landscape, Adam's boyish laughter trailing behind him.

"Show-off," Christian grumbled, edging Biscuit forward. "Don't mind him. Let's you and I take things nice and easy."

"Come on, OG," Lauren cooed to the horse, gingerly rubbing her sleek and shiny chestnut coat. "Let's go, girl."

Christian followed Lauren down the gently slanting hillside, enjoying the backside view. The sloping gave way to a vast expanse of flatland, and Lauren gradually increased OG's pace. Christian stayed just behind her. With each gentle jostle from the horse's gait, her ass lifted from the saddle, plump and rounded, accented by her tiny waist and bobbing ponytail protruding from beneath a cowboy hat.

In the middle of his borderline-inappropriate daydreaming, a series of quick movements caught his eye. A long, fast-moving whip snake slithered across the terrain. Old Glory sidestepped the snake and rose up. Her hooves pawed the air. The horse came back down with a vicious jolt and almost unseated Lauren.

"Lauren!"

In an instant Old Glory shed her years and ran like the wind. Lauren screamed as her body was jostled from side to side.

"Lauren, hold on!"

Christian spurred Biscuit on, trying to catch OG and grab the reins. Old Glory shifted right. Lauren's body went left and into the air, then landed on the ground with a sickening thud. Christian pulled Biscuit forward and missed her head by mere inches. He halted the horse, jumped out of the saddle and rushed to Lauren's body, motionless and twisted, beneath a clear blue sky.

Seven

Lauren felt as though she were in a tunnel far beneath the earth. In the distance there were voices that she heard but couldn't make out. Slowly, she came out of what felt like a fog and heard the words more clearly.

"Lauren, come on, beautiful. Wake up," Christian said.

Lauren heard hoofbeats, and then the muted sound of what she imagined was Adam dismounting Thunder and his handcrafted cowboy boots connecting with the hard earth.

"What happened?" Adam asked Christian.

"OG got spooked. It was a snake. Call the doctor, Adam," Christian said, pulling the blanket from under Biscuit's saddle and making a cushion for Lauren's head. "Have him meet me at my place."

She felt errant strands of hair being swiped away from her face as Christian spoke to her.

"Lauren, baby, please wake up."

She slowly opened her eyes. Squinting against the bright sunlight, she tried to focus on what was now a blurry view of Christian's concerned face. *What in the heck happened?* She tried to get up.

"No, don't move," Christian rasped, gently wiping damp tendrils off her forehead. "You may be hurt."

Lauren pushed away his hand, coughed and rose to her elbows. "I'm fine, just got the wind knocked out of me."

"Are you sure?"

"I think so." She moved her leg, which was not fine at all. "Ow!"

"I said don't move!" And then more calmly, "Where are you hurt?" Christian coddled her as gently as a swaddled babe, her head shielded in the crook of his arm as he helped her sit upright.

"I think my ankle is broken. It hurts like hell."

"We've got to get you out of here, sweetheart. I'm going to lift you up, okay? Place your stomach on the saddle. Then I'll pull your healthy leg around so we can lessen all movement of the other one."

He placed an arm beneath her legs. "No, Chris! Wait!"

"Trust me, I've got you. Okay?"

Lauren nodded. "Okay."

"Put your arms around my neck and hold on tight."

She did as instructed. Christian lifted her gently and laid her across the saddle. "I've got to steady your body while moving your leg, understand?"

Lauren acknowledged his question through gritted teeth.

"So you won't think that I'm trying to cop a feel."

She laughed and braced herself for his touch. Christian's hand splayed across her behind made her almost forget the pain. That she seemed unable to control her feelings had her convinced she'd already lost her mind.

Once she was safely mounted, with the blanket serving as padding for her injured ankle, Christian swung up behind her, pressed her back firmly against his chest and spurred Biscuit into action.

Lauren grimaced against the throbbing pain in her ankle that kept time with each instance that the horse's hooves touched the ground. She was going into a state of delirium. Had to be. There was no other way to explain that at a time when the ache in her leg was so severe she felt having it amputated without anesthesia would be less painful, she was keenly aware of the hardness of Christian's chest against her back, the feel of his arm on the side of her breast, and the way long, strong, sure fingers gripped her waist and held her firmly against him.

A flood of warmth pooled in her core, danced with the flames of pain shooting up from her ankle and set her entire body on fire. Why fight it? she thought as Adam's ranch house came into view. She closed her eyes and relaxed into Christian's embrace.

Seconds later, Lauren felt herself being gently lifted away from Christian's chest, while a sure pair of hands steadied her legs and ankle. She opened her eyes as Adam secured her legs with his arms and Christian effortlessly slid from the saddle while still maintaining a hand on her back.

"Careful, brother." The concern in Christian's urgently muttered command caused a pitter-patter in Lauren's heart. "Is the doctor—"

"Headed to your house right now. Not Dr. Simon, though. He recommended an orthopedic specialist. She's on the way."

"Let's get her in the car. Open the door and then go over to the other side to help me ease her in. Don't touch the right ankle. It might be broken."

Lauren wrapped her arms around Christian's neck and burrowed her head into his shoulder. The pain had ramped up considerably. Yet in the moment, her nostrils had the nerve to catch a whiff of Christian's cologne, a musky, smoky, spicy combination of sandalwood, bergamot and...was that patchouli? Damned if Lauren could help but reason that had she known this was the fastest way to end up in Christian's arms, she would have broken her foot Friday night!

Safely ensconced in the back seat of his SUV, Lauren felt the car turning around and speeding down the long road. From her visit to Victoria the previous day, she knew they were heading in the direction of the main house. Yet when the car pulled to a stop a few minutes later and she rose up to look around, the home-slash-architectural-wonder was one she hadn't seen before. One of three garage doors rose. Christian hopped out of the car and opened the back door, just as another car pulled up beside them.

"Where are we?" Lauren asked.

"My place," Christian said, scooping her up and effortlessly carrying her as though she weighed nothing at all. "The doctor is here, baby. You can relax now. Everything will be fine." He turned to the woman exiting a white sedan. "Doctor?"

"Yes. Dr. Burman."

"This way, please." With strong, sure strides Christian ate up the distance between the driveway and the side door inside the garage. As they neared it, the door opened.

"Mr. Breedlove!"

"Hi, Tara." And then to the doctor, Christian ordered, "Follow me."

As he passed by the woman holding open the door, Lauren took in the kind, worried eyes of a short older woman with long black hair. They continued down a hallway and up a short flight of stairs to the first-floor landing. Lauren caught glimpses of slate tile, marble, stainless steel and large paneless windows before they entered another hallway leading to a set of exquisitely carved black African wood double doors.

After placing his palm against a panel on the wall,

the doors opened into a master suite the size of Lauren's condo back home. He strode through a sitting area to a four-poster bed on a raised platform. As he gingerly laid her on a silky soft spread, she looked up, closed her eyes quickly and looked again. Instead of a luxurious beamed, vaulted or tray ceiling one might expect, the master suite's ceiling was made entirely of a tinted glass that let in the cloudless sky and the sun's colorful rays while shielding the room from its heat. If she died and went to heaven, she hoped she'd end up in a room like this.

"What can I get you, Doctor?" Christian asked.

"Only privacy," Dr. Burman responded, with the slightest of smiles as she placed a black bag on the bedside table and opened it.

"Oh, of course. I'll be right outside if you need me."

Dr. Burman began speaking before the door closed. "Hello... Lauren, correct?" She nodded. "We're going to have a look at that ankle, okay?" The doctor pulled out a pair of scissors. "I hope these aren't your favorite jeans. I'm going to have to cut them away to have a look."

"It's fine," Lauren replied, her jaw clamped tight against the pain.

The doctor's tone was casual, conversational, as she reached for the pants leg hem and began to cut. "On a scale of one to ten, how bad is the pain?"

"About a nine, I guess."

Lauren felt the doctor's gentle touch on her foot and calf. "The ankle is swelling quite a bit and beginning to bruise. Now, this is going to cause a bit of discomfort but I need to apply pressure on the affected area to determine the severity."

The doctor was quick and efficient. Once she finished examining the leg, she checked Lauren's vitals, as well. "At the very least you've experienced a severe sprain, and there may very well be a fracture of sorts. We'll need to get you in for X-rays to determine how extensive the damage is. Until then, I'm going to do a compression wrap of your ankle to provide stability and support and cold therapy packs to help decrease swelling. I'll also give you something for pain relief. Keep these pillows beneath the ankle so that it can remain elevated at all times. Other than that, stay off your feet as much as possible and get some rest. Do you have any questions?"

"If fractured, how long will it take to heal?"

"That depends on your body. In some cases a fracture can actually be better than a sprain because then you're dealing with bone instead of muscle, which can heal faster and easier. It feels as though your ankle is badly sprained. For now, just focus on staying calm and positive, knowing that with the Breedlove family you will receive the best possible care. If the condition worsens—more pain, further discoloration, continued swelling—we'll get you in for an X-ray tonight."

After wrapping the ankle and activating the ice pack, Dr. Burman disappeared to another part of the room and returned with a glass of water. She handed it to Lauren along with a pain pill and after briefly leaving the room, returned to Lauren's bedside. She helped remove the cut jeans and sweaty tee and provided her with a clean extra-large T-shirt from Christian's wardrobe room.

With the doctor's reassuring pat and a quiet goodbye, Lauren fixated on the colorful prisms on the glass overhead created by the sunrays as they danced their way west, and fell asleep within minutes. Hours later, groggily coming awake, she was filled with Christian's scent and the feeling of him in bed beside her—naked, hot and hard. She moaned, her arms encased in his embrace, something wrapped around her legs. She shifted to push the cover away from her foot and…

"Ow!"

Lauren's eyes flew open as pain shot through her body. Brow scrunched, she looked around as the sensual dream faded and cold, hard reality dawned. She was alone—not tightly ensconced in Christian's arms—and the bedsheets had somehow wound themselves around her.

Gingerly sitting up, she placed a pillow behind her and leaned against it while looking around. The lavishness and exquisite attention to detail in the room's design that she'd missed earlier were now breathtakingly evident—grays, tans and ivories, burnished metals, sleek, clean-lined furnishings and abstract art. There appeared to be several rooms; one she knew contained his wardrobe. Another she assumed was the master bath.

But there was more. Turning left, a profusion of color greeted her. On the bedside table was a bouquet of vibrant flowers: yellow calla lilies, orange roses and hot-pink daisies. Amid the blossoms and Hypericum berries was a small white envelope, her name scribbled across it. She pulled it from the holder and retrieved the note inside.

Hello, sleeping beauty: I hope you've rested well and are feeling better. Push the button beside you for whatever you need. Your pain medication prescription has been filled. The doctor sent along crutches. Don't use them. You'll heal faster by staying in bed. Tara is waiting to assist you with food, drink, whatever you need. I'll be home later.
CB.

She read the note twice, frowning at his presumptuousness in issuing orders even as she ran her finger over the authoritatively delivered promise that he'd be home later. Discreetly placed beside the table was the button he mentioned, one that she imagined would bring servants running, ready to attend to her every need.

What was it like to live this way, she wondered, with everything at your fingertips? A part of Lauren felt appalled at the idea, the other part could quite get accustomed to it. She nestled against the pillow, remembering her dream, imagining a lifetime with Christian beside her. She shifted her leg. A jolt of pain shot up from her ankle, reminding her why she was there. She sat up and consciously shut down the wistful meanderings.

She reached for the pad and pen on the table beside her and replied to Christian's acts of kindness. Then, after deciding what actions to take, she pushed the bedside button. Tara magically appeared. She carried a small plastic container that she set on a table. She removed a small pill cup and crossed to the bed.

"Are you in pain, Miss Lauren?" The housekeeper held out the small paper cup. "Here is your medication."

"Thank you, Tara, and please, just Lauren is fine."

"Oh, no, Miss Lauren. I couldn't. The title is a sign of respect."

Lauren shrugged. "Okay." Let the lady have it the way that she wanted. After today she'd likely not see her again. She reached for the glass of water on the nightstand and downed the pills.

"Are you hungry? Thirsty? Would you like help with a bath?"

"I'm fine, thank you. All I need is something decent to put on and a ride back to my house."

Tara's eyes briefly widened. "Oh, no, Miss Lauren. Mr. Breedlove gave explicit instructions that you are to remain here to be properly attended to."

Lauren's brows rose as images of how properly he could probably attend to her flashed through her mind.

"Thank Mr. Breedlove kindly, but it's only my ankle and it already feels better. I left a note so he'll know it was my call. Is there someone who can drive me, or should I call a cab?"

"That won't be necessary."

Both ladies turned as Christian sauntered into the room with the air of a boss and an expression that brooked no argument.

"Mr. Breedlove!" Tara stuttered. "I didn't expect you back until later."

"There was a change in plans." He moved to the edge of the bed and lifted the cold pack, now room temperature, from Lauren's ankle.

Tara hurried to the container she'd brought into the room. "Here is the new cold pack, Mr. Breedlove. I was just about to change it."

"Thank you, Tara." He spoke to the housekeeper but his eyes were on Lauren. "I'll take over from here."

"Yes, sir."

Once the housekeeper left the room, Christian walked over to place the used cold pack in the plastic container. After gently placing the fresh one on her ankle he said, "I thought my instructions for you were very clear—to remain here, in bed."

"And I thought my dad's name was Paul."

Lauren watched his eyes narrow and darken, the message within them unreadable. She kept her face neutral, but her insides shivered. This was her first encounter with his presidential persona, a man undeniably in charge, used to giving orders and having them followed. His autocratic demeanor and commanding tone were traits she was sure had felled lesser men. They moved her, too. But he wouldn't know it. She lifted a defiant chin and met his smoldering gaze.

The atmosphere in the room snapped, crackled and popped.

Christian's eyes held a devilish glint when he raised them to her. "You're being a lousy patient."

"A lousy houseguest, maybe, but I'm following the doctor's orders, Dr. Burman's instructions," Lauren emphasized, "as best as I can. She has an exceptional bedside manner."

"And I don't?"

A flippant answer died on her tongue, replaced by a quiet intake of breath that matched the slow, steady trail Christian made with his finger, from ankle to knee and back again. He walked to a chair, sat, and began removing his shoes.

"Are you saying my bedside manner needs improving?"

"I…"

Again, words failed her. Lauren could only watch as he rose from the chair and erased the distance between them. Without removing his khaki shorts or polo shirt he eased up on the bed and against the headboard and pulled her into his arms.

"Perhaps I'm out of practice," he whispered against her temple, before planting a kiss there, and then another. "Perhaps you being here is just what I need to… refine my skills."

He placed a finger beneath her chin. Lauren's head fell back against the arm that supported her. Since it had happened before, she thought she was ready for his explosive kiss—those pillow-soft lips and super-skilled tongue. But she wasn't, couldn't have been, or else the earth would not have tilted on its axis, along with her body as her tongue danced with his. A sigh of contentment escaped her lips as he brushed his cushiness against hers, kissed her cheek, then her neck. His hand moved down to her breast and cupped it. He flicked his thumb across her sensitive flesh and stroked her nipples, making them harden and her entire body yearn for more.

Her mind was willing, her heart open, her body oh so ready to receive everything that he had to give. But the pain medication was strong and chose this inconvenient moment to begin taking effect. She felt him ease away and off the bed.

"No…" She tried to pull him back to her, but he resisted.

"Not like this, my love. When we come together, I want you to remember everything that happens, and for the only haze to be that of our ardent desire. Right now you need rest and food."

"I'm not hungry."

"You need sustenance. I'll have the chef prepare and deliver a meal, and get someone to drive you home."

"Why not you?" Lauren mumbled through her fogginess.

He smiled, walked over and kissed her forehead. "Trust me, if I take you there, you'll get no rest at all."

A last kiss to the lips and Christian backed away. "Feel better, baby."

Tara helped her dress. A short time later, Lauren arrived at her front door, aided by a collapsible crutch and one of the estate's many employees. On her kitchen counter was a well-stocked basket from which wafted something delicious. She'd wanted nothing more than to stay in Christian's bed and have him rejoin her in it. Had it not been for the pain medication, it would have surely happened. Moments away from making love and once again, life had intervened. Maybe the universe was sending signs that a dalliance with Christian was not a good idea.

She already had one serious man problem. Perhaps she should focus on solving that issue before jumping into bed with another. Whatever the case, here, in her temporary abode, she'd have the space and the time to think more clearly. Because if she'd stayed in his home, the pain would have dissipated, her appetite would have returned, and Christian would most definitely have been on the menu.

Eight

Before leaving home and heading to work, Christian tucked Lauren and the events of the weekend into a mental box that he then pushed to the back of his mind. Compartmentalizing and single-minded focus were skills he'd unconsciously honed as a kid, ones that allowed him to master whatever challenge he faced and developed him into a brilliant businessman. Having just been promoted to president of CANN International, Christian was determined to stay focused on the myriad of moving parts in the family's ever-expanding empire. Even though Nicholas would continue to be a vital voice in the business, Christian knew that from now on the buck would stop with him.

So as he turned his pricey sports car into the private executive entrance of the hotel, his mind wasn't on yesterday when he'd returned home and found Lauren ready to flee. It wasn't on the mixed emotions he'd felt at having Lauren in his bed—hot, waiting and ready—and then realizing she'd just taken pain medication. He couldn't help but remember that had he not come home when he did, his bed would have been empty. Which brought up a few questions. Was she sending mixed signals, being a tease? How much of the desire she displayed was real, and how much was part of a grander scheme, perhaps the real reason she'd moved to Vegas to work with Mom? And maybe the most important question of all, why did he care?

Passing a mirror on the way to the boardroom, Christian stopped and took in his reflection with a critical eye. Today he wore an original design from his good friend Ace Montgomery's HIS collection. The tailored navy suit had been paired with a pale yellow shirt that highlighted his bronze skin and the blue, gold and silver patterned tie that bore the CANN logo. His jewelry was platinum but understated—square cuff links with a matching tie-pin and a deceptively simple watch.

Christian straightened his tie, ran a hand over his silky curls and then, convinced that his look was perfection, continued down the hallway. He wasn't vain, and while he'd walked the runway a time or two, he wasn't the style-conscious clotheshorse that fashion magazines often pegged him. But he was his mother's son. From their youth, Victoria had preached the importance of and connection between looking good and feeling good. Christian had listened and learned.

He reached the closed boardroom doors and, mentally pushing the on button, entered his first executive meeting as the corporation's president.

"Gentlemen, good morning!"

Hearty claps and a chorus of greetings followed him to the head of the table. He nodded in acknowledgment but didn't let the outward show of approval go to his head. He knew that at least two of the smiles were half-hearted at best and one was an outright lie. He was now the boss to men older, wiser and no doubt in their mind more deserving of the position.

"Thanks, everyone. I appreciate the support. Especially now, as I unfold plans for a vigorously ambitious building project, one that will be our most innovative and expensive to date. Let's get down to business."

He opened his laptop and connected it to a port on the table.

"As all of you know, CANN UAE was built at the onset of that country's push to become a playground for the wealthy. However, the window of unlimited opportunity and unbridled growth is quickly closing. For the past year, my advisers and I have been scouting the world for the best location of the next man-made paradise for the superrich, and I believe we've found it. More accurately, we've found the land where we want to create it. Any ideas?" He looked over at the adviser sitting at the table. "Not from you," he jokingly admonished.

The names of several locations were thrown on the table—from Sydney to Madagascar, to islands everywhere. As he listened, Christian pushed a button that turned the wall behind him into a screen and pulled out a pointer.

"All excellent ideas, guys, but none that are close. How about this choice?" He tapped his keyboard and on the screen came the outline of a country and one word, Djibouti.

"Where in the world is that?" half-hearted number one asked.

"Africa," another man answered.

"You've got to be kidding," said half-hearted number

two, his skepticism and dislike for Christian barely concealed. "No one's going on vacation to that part of Africa."

"A few years ago," Christian calmly countered, "that's what was being said about the Middle East, specifically the United Arab Emirates. Yet Dubai became a rich man's playground. In the next hour or two, the team leading this international effort and I will lay out the vision for this admittedly ambitious endeavor. I have not only faith in this vision but months of research and analysis behind me, and believe as did one wise farmer, and I paraphrase, if we build it correctly, the wealthy of the world will come. Why does the team so fervently believe this?"

Christian's nearly onyx eyes sparkled as he looked around the table. "Because we're CANN."

Back in Breedlove, Lauren also believed she could. She was confident in her abilities to properly assist Victoria, to make the upcoming fashion show the best that Vegas had ever seen. Even with a severely sprained ankle, as had been the news from her nine o'clock appointment with the podiatrist that Dr. Burman had recommended. It was a second degree sprain. The doctor assured Lauren that she'd be back jogging in four to six weeks.

Meanwhile, she'd gotten permission from Victoria to work from home and turned her dining room into an office. Sitting at the table, she fired up her laptop and opened a spreadsheet to chart out the tasks that needed completion and a timeline for making them happen. She'd just hobbled from the kitchen to the dining room with her microwaved tea when someone laid on the doorbell.

WTH?

"Coming!" She put down the mug, picked up the second crutch and crossed the room. She looked through the peephole. It was no one she recognized, but knowing how tight security was on the estate, she opened the door and would later pride herself on maintaining a solemn expression.

"Yes, may I help you?"

"Probably, Lauren, but I'm here to help you. Miss Vickie sent me over, said you could use an assistant, and from that muumuu-looking thing you're wearing, girl, I can see that she was right!"

"Excuse me?"

"I shall, and gladly, because when you got dressed this morning you didn't know me yet. Now can you let me in, because otherwise trying to work together with a screen door between us is going to be problematic."

Lauren listened to this rapidly delivered comment while taking in a man at least six feet tall, sharply dressed and flipping a perfectly coiffed shoulder-length bob away from a stunningly made-up face. As the teen girls she'd once mentored in DC would have said, his hair slayed and his face was beat. He stood in his truth with such confidence and authority that instead of being offended, she was humored and a little impressed. She unlocked the outer door and stepped back. The gentleman entered with a big smile and wide-open arms. He bent to embrace her.

"Hi, Lauren! I'm Frankie. It's so nice to meet you!"

"Me, too, I think." They both laughed. "When I spoke with Victoria this morning, she didn't mention anyone coming by."

"She told me I'd surprise you. Do you need help back to…" Frankie looked around. "Wherever you're sitting? This is nice," he continued without taking a breath, walking farther into the room and proving that if Lauren did need help she was on her own. "Miss Vickie's style is all over this place.

"Oh, I'm sorry," he continued as Lauren neared him. "Look at me seeing beauty and getting all carried away."

"Thank you, I'm fine." Lauren continued past him, noting the six-inch Louboutins giving Frankie extra height. "And what's wrong with my caftan?"

"Nothing that a Goodwill donation bin won't cure."

"Ha! You're funny."

"Laughter is the best medicine, child, and I'm trying to stay healthy. I see you're setting up shop in the dining room. How are you going to use those poster boards?"

"In lieu of a whiteboard, taped to the wall. Organizing projects on the board helps me stay organized in my mind. What is your skill set? By looking at you I'd guess it's the fashion world."

"That's one set, but don't let all of this fashion fabulosity fool you. I type eighty-five words a minute and can file papers better than my manicurist files my nails." He set a tote he carried on the table and pulled out a small laptop. "But yes, fashion is my passion. I love me some Ace Montgomery, honey. I don't know him personally but I have several friends in the industry, designers and models, male and female."

"Do you know London?"

"Ace's wife? Not yet. But if she comes to the show this weekend, I expect she and I will become the best of friends."

"That wouldn't surprise me at all. Would you like some tea?"

"No, thank you. Caffeine causes wrinkles."

"It's herbal, but thanks for the health information," Lauren finished sarcastically.

"Always grateful to be of service."

Said by Frankie so sincerely that Lauren laughed out loud. She took a seat at the table.

"Sit."

"Yes, ma'am."

Lauren wanted to get better acquainted with Frankie, who was *quite* a character, but later for that. There was a fashion show to finish coordinating. She'd promised Victoria an update at the end of the day, and with her newfound friend here to help her, Lauren was sure the report would be as good as her uplifted mood.

Nine

The week was a whirlwind of tweaking, adjusting and putting out fires. By Saturday night, Lauren and Frankie were best buds and as they stepped into the grand ballroom, redesigned as a Valentine-themed fashion fantasy, both knew the long hours and sleepless nights had all been worth it.

Grand chandeliers anchored yards—perhaps miles—of snowy white and fire-engine-red tulle covering the mass ceiling. Textured silk fabric adorned the walls. Five hundred cushioned chairs at tables for ten had been draped with designer organza tied with satin bows. Special risers had been installed to give each donor attending an unobstructed view. Dividing the room was a T-shaped runway that ran twice the length of a bowling lane, outlined with red Ecuadorian roses. Tucked in one corner was a ten-piece orchestra underscoring the fanciful scene with the classically romantic renderings of Tchaikovsky and Chopin, Puccini and Liszt. Lauren was almost moved to tears but couldn't be sure whether it was from the room's stunning beauty or lack of sleep.

"You did it, mama," Frankie whispered. Clearly, the room's beauty had moved him, too.

"*We* did it." Lauren turned toward him. "Seriously, I could not have done this without you. Which is why as of this moment you are officially off the clock and ordered to take your seat at table number two."

Frankie's jaw dropped. "Girl, don't play with me."

Lauren laughed. "I'm not."

"But what about you? I can't know you're still working and enjoy myself."

"Don't worry. I plan to join you. I'm just going to take one last walk-through and make sure everything's set."

Frankie gave Lauren an enthusiastic hug. "Thank you, girl. This feels like Christmas and the Fourth of July at the same time." He looked beyond Lauren's shoulder. "And Lord help me if I couldn't have some fireworks with that fine man right there!"

Lauren turned, expecting to see Ace or one of the male models. Instead, it was Christian heading her way.

"You go on and handle that, girlfriend," Frankie whispered. "I'm going to take my seat."

Lauren braced herself against the onslaught of desire guaranteed to erupt when their eyes connected. Now thankful for Frankie's earlier insistence that she dress to impress, she felt girlie, almost beautiful, in the silky kimono mini that draped her body and teased her skin. An unbidden image flashed through her mind—Christian's full, masculine lips replacing the fabric that kissed her flesh. As quickly as it appeared, she shut her mind against it. Christian was a tempting morsel. He was also Victo-

ria's eldest and unlike her father, Lauren had reversed
her plans to get entangled with a boss's son.

"Good evening, Lauren."

She nodded slightly. "Christian."

"You're looking stunning and a bit…uncomfortable?"

"No, not at all. I just…didn't plan to see you here."

"Where else would I be? The foundation is my mother's
passion but very important to all of us." Christian paused,
looked around. "Is this your handiwork?"

"I had help."

His eyes narrowed as they shifted from the room's
decor to Lauren's face. An expression as tantalizing as
it was unreadable sent a blast of heat to her core. What
was it about this guy, she wondered, that lit her body up
like a match?

"When it comes to glorious achievements, one should
never be coy."

"That's not my intention. I believe in giving credit where
it is due. A lot of people helped pull this day together, with
Frankie, my assistant for the show, topping the list."

Lauren finished speaking but Christian's eyes remained on her lips.

"What are you doing?"

"Remembering…"

One word drew dew from her feminine flower as Lauren was immediately transported back to last Sunday and
his master suite. His kiss. Those touches. A promise waiting to be fulfilled, but one that couldn't, shouldn't happen. For the umpteenth time she'd flip-flopped back to
her original position. Christian was off-limits. It wasn't
what she wanted, but being the professional that she was,
she knew it was the right thing to do.

"Yes, about that…"

Before Lauren could finish responding, they were interrupted by a harried assistant.

"Excuse me, Lauren. The social media campaign is crazy. Operators can't keep up. Can you come help us sort it out?"

"Sure." She turned to Christian, glad beyond words to be leaving his fine but mentally disruptive presence. "Enjoy the show."

Two hours later, the fashion show was over. Every piece of the puzzle had been placed to perfection. Wearing a heart-shaped dress made out of candy, celebrity model London Drake Montgomery had made the finale a showstopper, and Lauren's idea to auction off lunch dates with the male models had exceeded all expectations. Within minutes of the show ending, Victoria relayed great news. The show had set a record by raising more money than any other charity event to date.

Lauren was exhausted but giddy with excitement, not only because of the considerable buzz that had been created due to a social media marketing campaign she'd designed but also because Victoria had been gracious enough to fly Lauren's mother out for the event and put her up in one of the hotel's suites. Earlier there'd only been time for a quick hug, but they would spend the next two days together. Lauren had her luggage delivered there and had broken away from the crowd of well-wishers long enough to go and freshen up before joining Victoria, her mom and a few others for a late-night dinner.

It was the first time she was visiting Taste Test, one of ten restaurants spread throughout the CANN Casino, Hotel and Spa. She was more than ready. With her stomach having been in knots all day, Lauren hadn't been able to eat a thing. But now, with everything over and labeled a success, her appetite had come back in full force. Not even the throbbing ankle could wipe the smile off her face. The pain medication made her sleepy, and she didn't like taking drugs anyway. So she'd distracted herself from the ache with delicious food. Taste Test had received amazing reviews. She was about to judge for herself.

It was hard to be sexy on crutches. By the time she'd taken the elevator and navigated through the crowded hallways, Lauren almost wished she'd taken Frankie's advice to arrange for a blinged-out wheelchair and be chauffeured around. Lauren reached the hostess stand.

"Good evening! Bless your heart, can we get some assistance for you, a wheelchair perhaps?"

"No, I'm fine. I'm here for dinner with Victoria Breedlove. I'm Lauren Hart."

"Yes, Ms. Hart. Right this way."

Lauren followed the hostess down a hallway opposite the main dining room. There were a series of closed doors. She stopped at the first one on the right, gave a light tap and opened the door.

"Enjoy your evening."

"Thank you."

"There you are!" Victoria said, rising to greet her.

"I knew I should have gone up to help her," Faye said.

"No way." Lauren hugged Victoria. "Mom is staying for such a short time. I wanted you two to catch up."

"Sit there, darling," Victoria said, pointing to one of two empty chairs between Victoria and Faye.

Lauren complied and after a quick hug greeted the designer Ace, his wife London, and two foundation board members she'd met earlier in the day.

"Where's Frankie?" she asked, with a nod at the empty chair beside her.

"I have no idea," Victoria said.

"Perhaps trying his luck at a blackjack table," Ace offered.

"Not Frankie," Lauren countered. "He'd never spend money gambling when there are designer shops nearby."

While the rest of the table continued to chat, Lauren folded her crutches. She bent over to place them under the table, out of the way of the other guests, then heard the door open. Frankie, she thought, glad that Victoria had invited him to join them. Like Lauren, Victoria also knew he'd been a generous contributor to the show's overall success.

"My man!" Ace exclaimed.

She straightened, ready to laugh at Frankie's response, and her breath caught in her throat. It wasn't Frankie. It was the one and only man who could enter a room and change her temperature.

"Not this evening. You're the man," Christian replied, offering Ace a fist bump before kissing London on the cheek. "Good evening, everyone."

He waved at the board members, spoke briefly to Faye and continued around the table to Victoria. "Hello, gorgeous," he said, as he leaned down and kissed her cheek.

"Hi, son. Gorgeous is the one you're sitting beside. The most beautiful woman walking on crutches that I've ever seen."

"I agree with you," he replied, drinking in Lauren with his smoldering dark eyes.

"I have Ace and the HER collection to thank for that," Lauren said, referring to her kimono. "He and Frankie, who insisted on covering my bandage with the crystal-covered bootee."

"I'm kind of digging the bootee," London said. "You just might start a trend."

"Hello, beautiful."

Is it my imagination or did the room and everyone in it just fade away?

"Hello, Christian," Lauren answered.

He gave her cheek a whisper of a kiss, brushing his warm lips across her skin. Wreaking havoc on her body, as always.

"Congratulations on a job well done. The show was amazing."

"Thank you," she murmured softly. "I'm glad you enjoyed it."

"I wouldn't have missed it. Ace is my favorite designer."

Victoria feigned a cough. "I thought it was because mine was your favorite foundation."

"That goes without saying."

"Were you aware that tonight's fund-raiser was our most successful so far?" his mother asked.

"Really? Even more so than last year's golf tournament?"

"Absolutely," Victoria replied. "And we have Lauren's innovative and highly progressive marketing skills to thank for that."

"It was a team effort," Lauren said.

"To put on the affair indeed took a village. But your ingenious auctions for dates with the models and jewelry sold on social media allowed us to raise almost as much money from those who weren't in attendance as we did from those who purchased tickets and clothes."

"Interesting," Christian said, curiosity and a hint of admiration in his eyes. "Tell me more."

Lauren explained how after finding out about London's new jewelry line, she got the idea to present those items on social media, in limited quantities, to the highest bidder. Because of the short setup time frame, bids were limited to those within the United States. "Had it been opened internationally," she finished, "we would have easily doubled what was made."

Christian nodded. "I'd love to see the video."

"I'll send it to you."

"Perfect timing," Victoria announced as several servers arrived with the group's first course, each carrying two plates, and placed them down simultaneously. "Enough about CANN for one day. Let's talk about something really important."

She looked at London. "Like how someone who just had a baby four weeks ago can look absolutely fantastic!"

"Not to sound chauvinistic, but that sounds like a conversation for ladies' night out." Ace laughed at the immediate looks of indignation and hurried on to escape rebuttals. "Let's talk about something we can all participate in, like a trip to Paris by private plane. I heard someone at the table just got one."

Christian sat back, a smile barely concealed. "That's the rumor."

"More than a rumor," said one of the board members. "My husband shared pictures with me last week. He'd gone online and found the model. Very nice."

"Thank you, Ally. It was an incredible gift and you're all invited to join me on a trip I'm taking next week. It's not Paris, though."

"Where?" Ally asked. "Italy? I've never been but always wanted to. I hear it's so romantic, and with my divorce almost final…"

She let the sentence fade as imaginations took over and the titters increased.

"Not sure that where I'm going next week you'll find romantic," Christian said, pausing for dramatic effect. "I'm going to Djibouti."

"Da-booty?" Faye repeated, and the table laughed.

"Ja-booty, Mom," Lauren corrected with an indulgent smile. "It's a small country in the Horn of Africa, strategically positioned to be a commercial, military and shipping hub."

Christian wasn't the only one looking at her with amazement. Lauren wasn't used to being the center of attention but when in her wheelhouse of business, PR and marketing, her confidence soared.

"Last year I worked for a client doing business there," she explained. "I was hired largely because I could create his marketing materials in French, one of the country's three official languages."

"Have you been there?"

Lauren shook her head. "No, Christian. Just lots of research online."

"Did you hear that, Christian?" Victoria interjected. "Lauren speaks fluent French and is an expert on the country that you're scheduled to visit."

"Yes, Mom. I heard. And yes, that is impressive."

"I wouldn't exactly call myself an expert," Lauren demurred.

"Perception is reality," Victoria countered. "And from where I'm sitting, you have assets that could greatly benefit not only the CANN Foundation, but the corporation as well."

The servers returned with the evening's second course, and the conversation went in another direction as London and Ace regaled the table with untold tales of the fashion world.

While all eyes were on them, Christian leaned over and whispered, "You can run, but you can't hide."

"Who's running?"

"Earlier, it appeared that you were."

"I didn't run. I was called away. Why would I want to run from you?"

"That's what I'm trying to find out."

"I'm not running," she repeated, more forcefully this time.

His chuckle, soft and deep, made her core quiver.

"I'm beginning to think that you're a tease, Lauren Hart."

"I am not."

"Prove it."

The very words she'd used the day he returned the bracelet came back to haunt her. London saved Lauren. She asked a question about DC. Later, Lauren would have been hard-pressed to remember anything else talked about at the table, her body in sensory overload at Christian's nearness. His scent, that deep, husky voice, the way his leg casually brushed against hers when he shifted, the manner in which his eyes floated over her body with a subtle intensity. How did he do that? How did he manage to at times look totally uninterested and in the next moment fix her with a quick, ardent gaze that got her wildly aroused?

She sighed. The only thing more delectable than him at the table was her third-course choice of a grilled cedar plank swordfish. The roasted zucchini and cherry tomatoes that accompanied the dish caused a gustatory orgasm, and the black-and-white truffle creamy wild rice on which the fish rested was so decadent she could have licked the plate. Still, when her mother begged off dessert citing fatigue, Lauren was grateful. It had been a long day, and trying to maintain a casual indifference toward the hottie beside her was like another job. Besides, her mother was leaving soon. She needed mommy time.

Christian reached for his phone and passed it to her

beneath the table. "Type in your number," he commanded in a low tone meant for her ears only. When she hesitated, he continued. "For the video link," he explained. "Unless you're afraid of how much you want me, knowing that one night together might not be enough."

Lauren snatched the phone, hurriedly typed in her number, hugged Victoria and said goodbye to the table. Christian's parting words played on mental repeat. She was chagrined at how accurate his arrogant assessment was. Yes, she wanted him. Yes, she was afraid. But Lauren ran from wannabe fiancés and desperate fathers, not from his type of danger. Christian had asked her to prove that she wasn't a tease. Soon, he'd get just what he asked for.

Ten

Once out of the private dining room, Lauren finally acquiesced to the use of a wheelchair, which Faye insisted on pushing. They reached the suite and while she'd been in it earlier, Lauren was newly impressed. Earlier her focus had been on a quick change and food. Now she had a chance to take in and appreciate the room's simple grandeur, if there could be such a thing. While being wheeled to the suite where her mother was staying, Lauren's phone dinged. Christian.

Let's link up. Starting with the video...

She smiled, sent the promotional video from the fundraiser and set her phone to silent. The next several hours were for her and her mother alone.

"This suite is truly beautiful," Lauren said from the living room. She rose from the wheelchair, tossed one crutch down and used the other to walk over and take in the view.

"I told Victoria not to make a fuss over my visit, but she insisted I stay here."

"Next time you should plan to stay longer, and at my place."

"Your place?"

"Well, technically the home belongs to the Breedloves, but it's mine for now."

"Yes, Victoria told me. You're under contract until mid-July."

Faye joined Lauren and peered out floor-to-ceiling windows that showcased the length of the neon-lit Strip. Then she turned to her daughter.

"You look good, dear. Las Vegas seems to agree with you."

"Getting away from the stress of Ed and Dad's demands sure does."

"Is that it? The miles between here and Maryland?"

Lauren ignored her mother's knowing smile. Since the women were best friends, she was sure Victoria had told Faye all she thought she knew about what was happening between Lauren and Christian. She peeked into one of two spacious bedrooms before hobbling over to a low-slung tan couch and plopping down. She reached for the remote and turned on the television. Several local stations had covered the fund-raiser. She was curious how it would be shown on the news.

Faye followed her over. She sat in a matching chair, ran her hand over the deluxe silk velvet and lovingly eyed her daughter.

"You must be exhausted."

"I am, and happy my first event as Victoria's personal assistant is in my rearview mirror."

"It was fantastic, darling. Victoria went on and on about how well you did. You should be very proud."

"I never could have done it without my assistant, Frankie."

"Perhaps he can take over when you leave."

"Or perhaps this temporary move will become permanent."

"You can't really mean that."

"Yes, Mom, I do. For the first time in months I'm not being badgered. I can't tell you how good that feels."

"That's largely because your dad believes you'll be back home soon."

"What has he told you about this sudden friendship with Ed, encouraging us to get married? His explanation about Ed coming from such a good family and me getting older...he's never been interested in my personal life. It just doesn't add up."

"The Millers are a good family," Faye offered.

Lauren was incredulous. "Are you taking his side?"

"No. It's just...never mind."

"Mom, what is it?"

"Let's talk about it tomorrow, Lauren. It's been such a wonderful day."

Lauren reached for the remote and muted the TV. Suddenly the segment airing about the fashion show didn't matter as much as she'd thought. "Mom..."

"You can't breathe a word of this to your father. He's such a proud man. But given how this could impact your future, you have a right to know."

Taking in the seriousness mixed with sadness that was her mother's expression, Lauren's stomach dropped. She may have the right to know, but did she want to?

"I know how hard your father worked to keep his business going, how much he struggled."

"I think we were all aware of it," Lauren said softly. "At one point he was working seven days a week."

Faye nodded. "What I didn't know is that he took out a few loans during that time."

"From Ed?"

"Not initially. Lauren, he mortgaged the house."

"Oh, no!"

"Twice."

Lauren covered her mouth to stifle a gasp. Furnishing and decorating the five-bedroom, three-bath home in Maryland's upscale Brandywine neighborhood had filled up those early months and eased Faye's dismay about leaving friends and family on the West Coast behind. Being forced to leave the home would be devastating. The sadness she saw in her mother's eyes took on new meaning.

"I still don't understand Ed's connection."

"I'm getting to that. Paul had known his banker for years and was assured that they'd work with him until he'd paid back the money. But a little more than six months ago Liam, the loan officer who was also Paul's friend, got promoted. The new officer was not as lenient as Liam had been and demanded the long-overdue loan be immediately repaid in full."

"And Ed lent Dad the money." The sickening scenario became crystal clear. It was about that time that Ed had called and tried to get back together. He'd obviously used the loan as leverage to get her father on his side. Except her mother's tortured expression suggested there was more to the story.

"Oh my gosh, Mom. You look so worried. How much did he borrow?" Lauren asked this despite the fact that she doubted the five-figure amount in her savings account would cover what her dad owed.

"I don't know exactly, but given that our home is now worth half a million I'd say it's a sizable amount. And like the new banker, Ed wants all of it now unless you two get married."

Several minutes passed as Lauren digested the news. "There's got to be another solution. I mean, I know how much you love your home and I'd hate for you to lose it, but... I can't be with Ed. He's not a nice guy."

Faye's eyes narrowed as she studied her daughter. "Did he hurt you, Lauren?"

"No, not in the way you're thinking. Ed was never physically violent. But sometimes it's the verbal and emotional abuse that leaves the bigger scars."

Faye reached over and placed a comforting hand on Lauren's arm. "Nothing is worth your unhappiness, sweetheart, and nothing is worse than being in a loveless marriage."

"But that home means everything to you. What if you lose it?"

Faye sat back, her lips a thin line of determined strength. "I'll regret it, but I'll live."

The conversation didn't last much longer. Totally drained, Lauren stumbled into the bedroom, stripped naked and fell into bed. In the dark quiet came the drone of a vibrating cell phone, the one that she'd earlier silenced. Fumbling for her purse on the nightstand, she pulled out the phone and checked the messages. Three of them were from Christian, the last one a question that for Lauren was a total surprise.

Will you come with me to Djibouti? Your fluent French will be an asset and not only was Mom's suggestion right on, she's already approved your time away from the foundation.

With Faye's latest revelation fresh in her mind, Lauren knew what her answer would be. She needed money, and a plan, to help dig her parents out of their financial troubles. Perhaps this trip would give her time to think one up. She replied without hesitation.

Yes.

It would be morning when she'd see Christian's simple response. A smiley face and a thumbs-up.

Eleven

When off work, the average worker rushed to get away from their job. But when employed by the best hotel in the world, with the finest accommodations and entertainment in the city, there was often no hurry to leave. At 9:00 p.m. on a Wednesday night, Christian was still at CANN, entertaining a high-rolling client and prince from Brunei, along with his brother Noah, who worked in international sales, and Greg Chapman, the department's VP. They'd dined at Chefs, the über-exclusive restaurant that catered to their high rollers and other 1-percenters. It held only twenty tables and boasted menus without prices. The unspoken rule was, if you had to ask, you couldn't afford it.

Now that the meal was complete, the group relaxed in the members-only club near Chefs, where corporate executives took businessmen wanting to be away from the commoners' prying eyes, drink vintage liquor and enjoy stellar entertainment. They sipped pricey cognac from crystal snifters and listened to a band playing a folksy kind of neo soul, fronted by a woman whose voice reminded Christian of the singer Sade. He checked his watch and signaled the bartender to put the table's bill on the company tab.

Standing, he stifled a yawn and leaned toward the prince. "Gentlemen, it is a pleasure doing business with you, but I have an early-morning international flight, so I will take my leave." He addressed the other men at the table. "Noah, Greg, good night."

It wasn't until he neared the door that he realized someone else he knew had been enjoying the room's heady ambiance. Chloe stood with the look of someone well aware of her beauty, but for Christian, she wore a dress too revealing, boobs too surgically enhanced and a smile too seductive, especially in this room. When she'd asked for a card key to the private lair, he'd given her one without a second thought. Now he wondered whether or not that had been a good idea.

"Hey, handsome."

He allowed a light hug. "You know that coming in here alone isn't wise. Women who do so usually have an agenda. The men might get the wrong impression."

Chloe wriggled her eyebrows. "Or the right one."

"All right, then. Good night."

"Wait up. I'm leaving, too."

Lucky me. Christian headed toward the elevator, the private one that would take him directly to the executive lot and his car. Chloe stayed beside him.

"Where are you going?"

"What, no time to drive a friend to her car?" she purred.

"You're not valeted?"

"Yes, but that shouldn't matter."

"Not tonight, Chloe." Christian pushed the button. "It's been a long day. Once in my car I only want to stop for traffic lights or an opening gate."

The elevator arrived. Christian stepped in, standing near the door to block Chloe's entrance.

"In that much of a hurry to get home to your latest toy? It's been a couple weeks. I'd have thought you would have tossed her away already."

Christian knew what she wanted. Info. Details. From the time he'd met her when they were ten, it was her world and those around her were blessed to be in it. But just like she knew he could see through her fakery, had gotten that lesson in the very worst way, she should have known that like all of the other Breedloves, Christian kept it real. And private. Behind the bedroom door.

"Good night, Chloe."

He stepped back so the door would close, then thought about her comment regarding Lauren. *Discarded?* Hardly. That precious plaything hadn't even been unwrapped. But soon.

Back at the Breedlove estate, Lauren walked into the guesthouse's master suite closet and tried to act as though it were every other day that she flew to the other side of the world on a private plane with the handsomest man in the Western US. Aside from meeting with Victoria for most of the day, this was the first time her thoughts went to anything other than what she'd learned from Faye's visit. Her father, cornered. Her mother, quietly distraught. Her nemesis, determined. Her life, upended.

Oh, how she wished she had a million bucks lying around, or whatever amount was needed for repayment. She'd have the money converted to pennies, placed in a dump truck and delivered to Ed so that he could be buried in them. Lauren had never been a gambler but more than once since she'd left home she'd had flights of fancy involving slot machines with million-dollar payoffs or driving to purchase a lottery ticket just beyond the state line. If Lady Luck was going to strike, it had better happen quickly. Faye had tried to make the truth less foreboding, but Lauren had known Ed for a decade. He was ruthless and selfish. Dad was in over his head.

She had no doubt that Ed was ramping up the pressure, turning the screws, forcing a decision to be made quickly. No matter how her mother tried to paint a rosier picture, the truth of the matter was that only a wedding ring stood between her dad and mom losing their forever home, maybe more. Lauren wouldn't put it past Ed to threaten her dad's livelihood. A man she detested held the ring, and the finger he wanted to place it on was hers.

Faye had assured Lauren that a house wasn't worth her unhappiness, but could she live with knowing her decision resulted in her mom losing that dream home, and her dad maybe losing his job?

Trying to force back the thoughts that had led to pounding headaches two days in a row, she pulled several items from their hangers and reached for the handle of her luggage. After tossing the items she'd chosen on the bed, she walked to the beautifully crafted armoire that anchored the wall opposite her bed and gathered her sexiest lingerie.

Instead of her usual attempts to push away thoughts of Christian, tonight she welcomed a flood of them into her mind and allowed herself to imagine ignoring good sense and being with him. Tomorrow, they were boarding his private jet and flying to Africa! While not sure of what phase they were in with the project, she doubted they'd be traveling alone. Most likely there'd be a few other executives, maybe an assistant or two, other investors...who knew? Maybe one roll in the hay with the guy and Christian would be out of her system. With that in mind, she picked out her naughtiest undies in case a spontaneous seduction occurred. After returning back to the States would be soon enough to contemplate her nightmare. But for the next several days, while traveling with Christian, she'd allow herself to dream.

The phone rang. She checked the ID.

Dad. Great. Dream over.

Lauren started not to answer. But her curiosity about what was being cooked up between her dad and Ed trumped her desire to leave all of her problems behind and head straight to the plane. She pressed the speaker button and continued to pack.

"Hi, Dad."

"Hello, Lauren."

He sounded formal, official, the same as he would while addressing a client. The history was different, but when it came to personality, Ed and her father were a lot alike.

"Faye said you wanted to speak with me regarding my project with Ed. I was disappointed to learn that she'd divulged my personal business. It is none of your concern."

"Good, then I expect you to stop campaigning on Ed's behalf. I will not marry him."

"Ed loves you dearly, as do I, and wants to build a solid foundation that will benefit generations for both of our families."

"There doesn't have to be a marriage for that to happen."

"But Ed is in love with you. It's what he wants."

"What about what I want?"

"And what is that?" Lauren bit her lip to remain silent. Given that there were few secrets between her parents, her dad most likely knew about Christian. "Promise me you won't do anything stupid, Lauren."

"I've got to go. Bye, Dad."

"Lauren!"

It was the first time in her life she'd ever defied him. But Lauren wasn't about to make a promise that she wasn't sure she could keep.

An unexpected knock at the door caused her to flinch, a sign of just how badly the conversation with her father had put her on edge. She hoped it was Frankie, always good for a laugh or lending a compassionate ear. Her smile was faint yet hopeful as she peeped through the hole.

"Hey, you," she said after opening the door, batting away frustrating tears.

Christian stepped inside and took her into his arms. A diversion was just what she needed.

Twelve

It wasn't what he'd intended to do, but Lauren looked as though she could use a hug. He would have ended it there, but when she glided her arms around his neck, wearing a skimpy top and boy shorts, reminding him of a butterscotch bar, what could he do but accept the invitation to cuddle? Then when she pressed her body into him and thrust her tongue into his mouth all Christian could think was...*well, damn!*

Christian deepened the kiss. He loved kissing, always had. It was an art he'd purposely perfected and growing up had practiced every chance he got. Lauren's kisses were magical, and the thought of her becoming proficient the way he did made him want to punch every guy she'd ever dated. Their mouths fit together as though hers had been made especially for him. But had it? Were those delectable lips now sliding down the side of his face to his neck a gift...or a weapon?

He slowly pulled away from her. "That was some greeting."

Lauren stepped back to let him in. "I won't apologize for it, but I got carried away."

"Are you all right?"

"Not really." Lauren reached for the crutch leaning against the wall, crossed to the bar counter and perched on one of the stools.

"Do you want to talk about it?"

"No." She looked at his lips.

"Is there anything I can do to make you feel better?"

"You can use that irresistible mouth of yours for something besides talking."

Without a word, he swept Lauren up into his arms and walked them into the bedroom.

He gently laid her on the bed and followed her down. Lauren's movements were urgent, but he slowed the pace, kissing every exposed piece of skin. He felt pebbling beneath his chest and rose up just enough to lift up her top and give a nipple a nibble. Laving the darkened circle barely discernible in the darkness, he thought of truffles and bonbons, only Lauren was sweeter. She moaned, and he kissed the other peak, a mere flicker really, a promise that he'd be back. Then he was back at her mouth, and this time he meant business. He pressed his tongue inside her warm, moist cavern. Their tongues danced and dueled and got to know each other.

"Chris." His name floated on a whisper into his ear. She moaned again, pulled off her tank top and reached for his belt. Christian felt himself harden and lengthen, and no longer cared to slow things down. They'd take their time on round two. And there *would* be a round two. He'd make sure of that.

Placing a knee on each side of her, he sat back and

stared at her perfectly shaped, weighty globes, then gripped the waistband of her shorts and began to pull. Lauren rose up, her eyes dark with desire. She ground her hips a little.

Sexy-ass minx.

He eased the shorts over her hips, smiling at the patch of curly black fur covering her treasure. Some guys made a big deal of a girl being shaved, but for Christian that was overrated. If that was the woman's choice, cool, but sometimes a mass of soft ground cover meant she hadn't recently prepared it for anybody, that she hadn't been ravished in a while. Lauren said she hadn't recently dated, and not that it mattered, but he believed her. The thought of a snug welcome and rhythmic friction lengthened Christian's erection even more.

Propping his hands on her knees and careful of her ankle, he coaxed her legs apart and took a long, slow dip into her dewy valley. The long moan emitted from the back of her throat let Christian know he was onto something that Lauren liked.

A lot.

That meant he couldn't half step. He needed to do the job right. So he shifted them until he could lie comfortably between her legs and spread apart her folds with his tongue. Licking, lapping, he tasted her essence, massaged her into a hardened pearl. He spread her wider, tasted deeper, raised his hands and cupped her breasts. She ground her hips against his face. Encouraging his direction. The move made him so dizzy with desire, he was about to burst. Sliding off the bed, he shimmied out of his pants and reached for his wallet in one smooth motion. He quickly tore open the foil packet and sheathed his engorged member. He climbed on the bed and held his body aloft.

"Are you ready, baby?" he whispered.

"I'm so ready," she replied.

"Then let's do this."

He aimed his ample appendage at her entry of ecstasy and connected with her in the deepest way possible with one...slow...continuous thrust.

Then the party started for real. Him plunging, retreating and plunging again. Her lifting her arched body, wanting him again and again. And when she squeezed her inner walls, tightly, it was Christian's turn to moan. He eased his hands beneath what could only be described as the juiciest booty, squeezing her softly as he branded her core.

"Oh my goodness," she gasped as her hip motion increased. Then more sounds, high-pitched, unintelligible, until her nails dug into his back as she went over the edge. Just in time, too, as Christian was also at his zenith. He plunged harder, faster, backward, forward, then shouted his release before collapsing on the bed beside her.

"What just happened?" Lauren asked in wonder, still catching her breath.

"Whatever it was," Christian muttered as he reached over and pulled her against him, "I cannot wait for it to happen again."

He didn't have long to wait. The second time was slower, languid, like blue-lights-in-the-basement, straight-ahead jazz. They showered together, and Christian received an unexpected treat. Turns out that kissing wasn't the only thing Lauren did well with her mouth.

Later, clean and sated, they cuddled beneath a sheet, watching the candle Lauren lit between rounds one and two flicker against the wall.

He stroked a finger across her shoulder, kissed her temple. "Do you feel better?"

"Infinitely so," she murmured. "You?"

"I'm not sure, to be honest. I might need rehab."

He felt Lauren's head rise off the pillow. "Rehab? Why?"

"Because your love is addicting and I could get hooked."

"Oh, Lord."

They laughed, hugging, before Lauren perched against the headboard. Christian rose up, too.

"So you haven't been with anyone in a while, huh?"

Lauren chuckled. "How could you tell?"

"I could tell."

"What about you?"

"Nothing serious, not lately. I have a few friends with a clear understanding. We're casual, getting together to have a good time. That's about it."

"Have you ever thought about getting married?"

Christian ran a hand over the sheet as he pondered the question. "I did, once."

"What happened?"

"Someone I'd dated but no longer dealt with came back and messed it all up."

She arched a brow. "You cheated with her?"

"No, but that's how she made it look."

"Wow, that's jacked up."

"Totally."

Lauren could feel his eyes searching for her in the darkness.

"What about you?"

"What *about* me?"

"Ever thought about getting taken off the market?"

"Taken off the market? Ugh! What am I, an egg?"

"Well, technically speaking…"

She hit him with a pillow. Talk lessened after that and

then ended altogether. They fell asleep, spooning, Lauren clutching Christian's big, strong arms around her. They woke up, hours later, the very same way.

Thirteen

Las Vegas was known for attracting the world's finest in the art of illusion and wizardry. Christian had sat in premium seats and seen the best of the best. But he'd never experienced the kind of magic that had happened last night between him and Lauren. He didn't want to overthink it or ruminate on what had happened before he arrived last night.

She'd pulled back a bit this morning, more guarded, less carefree. Clearly she didn't want to put a label on what was happening. Heck, he didn't either. But Christian knew one thing for sure. Even with the level of heat between last night's high-thread-count Egyptian sheets, the passion between them was just beginning to burn.

After a quick trip to Dr. Burman's office, Christian and Lauren headed straight to the airstrip. Their luggage had already been loaded, the plane had been checked, and they were ready for takeoff. Most of their time together had been with each of them handling last-minute business before leaving the country—Lauren on her tablet, Christian on his phone. But now, as they settled into the first two seats with Lauren's ankle propped up on a padded stool, a light breakfast ordered and the Gulfstream taxiing down the runway, Christian reached over and squeezed her hand.

"You okay, beautiful?"

"I'm fine, especially since speaking with Victoria this morning. Frankie is going to work in my absence so I don't feel that I'm leaving her in a lurch."

"And your ankle? There's really no pain?"

"None at the moment, thanks to this functional yet ugly thing."

Lauren lifted the leg that the doctor had outfitted with a sleek black bionic ankle brace and wriggled her freshly painted toenails.

"I don't know," he replied, his voice as silky as the leg he now squeezed, peeking out from the thigh-high slit in Lauren's maxi. Knowing that heaven awaited mere inches beneath the fabric almost made him go hard. "Your boot is kind of sexy."

"Frankie would kill me if he knew I'd matched this dress with such plainness."

"I'll take care of it." Christian reached for his phone.

"Who are you calling?"

"The other passengers coming on this trip."

"I thought you said it would be just the two of us."

"I said it would be only you and me in Djibouti. But we've got a couple slackers wanting to bum a ride to London."

Lauren frowned, obviously confused.

Just then the captain—not Jesse but an equally capable and more formal young pilot named Dennis—came over the intercom.

"An official good morning to you, Mr. Breedlove, Ms. Hart. You've picked a great day to fly across the pond. We've reached our cruising altitude of forty thousand feet. All the way into Hayward there's nothing but golden sunshine and blue skies so sit back, relax and enjoy the ride."

"Hayward?"

"Northern California, near San Francisco."

Lauren's eyes lit up. "Ace and London are coming with us?"

"They are indeed."

An hour later the plane descended and scooped up Mr. and Mrs. Montgomery. While London and Lauren settled on the couch and Christian gave Ace a tour of the plane, the ground crew loaded their luggage.

London reached into a designer tote and pulled out a sock dipped in crystals. "Voila!"

Lauren laughed out loud. "You've got to be kidding! Frankie made the glittery bootee I wore to the show. I didn't know they could actually be purchased."

"They can't be. That's an original, darling. Whipped up just for you."

"No way. Christian just called you, what, half an hour ago?"

"How long do you think it takes to dip a piece of apparel in fabric glue and roll it in Swarovski?"

"Is that what you did?"

Now it was London who chuckled. "Hardly. Ace called one of the guys at the shop who worked his magic and met us here."

"Wow, that makes me feel really special. Thanks."

"No, thank you. A version of what you're holding will be in our next collection. Hey, maybe we'll use you as the model." London lifted her chin as Frankie would. "You'll be fabulosity, sweetness."

"Oh my goodness, the moment Frankie sees this he'll expire on the spot. In fact, you should get him to model for you. Wait! I just thought of something."

"What?"

"Where's the baby?"

"Our little princess left with her nanny and the staff last night. They'll be there and have the house ready when we arrive. Speaking of, how long will you be in London? We've got some great friends there that we'd love you to meet."

Christian and Ace joined them in the sitting area. The plane took off and the party started. That London and Ace were on board with them could not have made Lauren happier. She didn't regret what happened last night. In fact, she couldn't wait for it to happen again. But having sex with Christian couldn't help but complicate a situation that the conversation with her dad made even more convoluted. A situation that no matter how much she wished, seemed to not be going away.

Later, she told herself, as the flight attendant brought out mimosas made with freshly squeezed orange juice and a ridiculously expensive bottle of Krug vintage brut.

For the next ten hours they ate, drank and, for Lauren, experienced shoptalk at a whole other level. She marveled at how London, Ace and Christian discussed billions and trillions the way average people talked about twenties and tens. The slackers, Lauren learned, would play an intricate role in the playground of the rich that Christian envisioned in Africa, with a designer house of Ace's fashions anchoring a sprawling mall and London's

A-list celebrity connections purchasing properties and making the man-made islands like pricey, limited-edition baubles that only the wealthiest and luckiest could attain.

She watched the ease with which these friends did business together and couldn't imagine the same relaxed camaraderie between Ed and her dad. The pilot announced the plane's initial descent. The couples returned to their seats and buckled up for landing, and Lauren snuggled into the comfort of Christian's warm embrace.

"Good idea, baby," he whispered, his breath hot and wet against her ear.

"What?"

"Getting your rest. You're going to need it."

She shifted her head to look at him. "Is that so?"

"That's *so* so."

"Why? What's going to happen later?"

He pulled her closer to him. "It involves getting you wetter for me tonight than you were last night, and then taking my time to lick you dry."

His plan was already working. Lauren squeezed her thighs together against the pulsating flesh.

"Stop being a bad boy," she cooed, nestling deeper into his arms.

He kissed the top of her head. "Not a chance."

For a second her shield slipped, and Lauren wondered how it might feel to spend a lifetime in this luxury, night after night in the protection and passion of Christian's strong arms. Just as quickly the fantasy dissipated, replaced by a vision of Ed's cocky smirk and the memory of her dad's somber plea. Christian was a stellar deflection from what she faced once back stateside. But Lauren held no delusions that he'd ever be anything more than that.

They touched down at London's Luton Airport in the wee hours of the morning. After customs personnel had boarded the plane and quickly cleared them, the foursome dashed through a steady drizzle to a waiting car. As they neared the driver hopped out, opened the door and ushered them inside before handling their luggage. London nestled her head against Ace's shoulder and closed her eyes. Then, in a universal man move, Ace and Christian settled into a conversation about the car transporting them, a Rolls-Royce Phantom with seats that faced each other and leather so soft it cupped the body like a blanket.

Lauren was glad to not have to engage in conversation. The plane had landed but parts of her still floated above the clouds. Remembering Christian's naughty plans for the night ahead, her core quivered and her nether lips pulsed. Just thinking of his tongue once again inside her made every part of her body react. Nipples pebbled. Nub engorged. She was shaky and dewy and out of control, and even though bouts of drowsiness and jet lag accompanied the time change, all she wanted was Christian, demanding and hard.

A half hour later, the driver pulled up to the Sanderson Hotel in Berkenshire. Ace and London had invited them to stay at their home, but considering that they'd been on a plane for ten-plus hours and her namesake city was ninety miles away, Christian declined the invite. Lauren believed there may have been another reason, that he wanted what she wanted.

She was right.

Within minutes of the driver bringing in their luggage before tipping his hat and wishing them good-night, Christian and Lauren tumbled into bed. She wore nothing but her sexy bionic brace, which was covered by London's thoughtful gift, on the ankle Christian thoughtfully propped up with pillows before sheathing himself, sliding behind her and thrusting himself into her waiting warmth. He moved slowly and rhythmically, branding her soul, his fingers keeping the same pace sliding over her nub. Her orgasm was deep and delicious, intensely satisfying, and just as her eyelids fluttered shut she decided soothing sex with a master beat melatonin any night of the week.

Fourteen

A text Christian received when he and Lauren awakened Saturday morning necessitated a change in plans. He'd been invited to meet the following day with members of the president of Djibouti's administration and a small group of businessmen. Knowing the importance of establishing and maintaining excellent relations with the country's political structure, he cancelled their plans for joining Ace and London for dinner at Restaurant Gordon Ramsey, and had their pilot make flight plans that would put them in Djibouti in time for a good night's sleep before the business meeting.

It would be his first return to the country since purchasing his own island, one of the smaller, more pristine in the Indian Ocean, his first time seeing the home he'd designed, with a mini golf course as the backyard and a pool on the roof.

Their flight arrived in Djibouti around one a.m. and

instead of nonstop lovemaking as had happened in England, Christian and Lauren got a good night's sleep. After his business meeting later that morning, the couple toured the capital, Djibouti City. Christian loved introducing Lauren to the local cuisine and sharing what he'd learned of the country through extensive research and his many visits there.

The Republic of Djibouti, located in the Horn of Africa, bordered by Eritrea, Ethiopia and Somalia, was not the type of country most would consider as a possibility for a vacation paradise. But it fit Christian's vision perfectly, especially the islands off the coast of Djibouti in the Gulf of Tadjoura. The paradisiacal enclave of the Indian Ocean boasted an abundance of pearl oysters, extensive coral reefs and privacy. Before, he could only imagine the love nests that could be created for the rich and famous craving discretion. Now, with Lauren beside him, what he'd envisioned had come to life.

He looked at her now, golden body shimmering against the water, bathed in the light of a waning sun. Curly wet hair splayed across her shoulders and down her back. The rounded ass he loved so much bobbing out of the water like an apple ripe for biting. But he resisted and instead took in her pensive expression, and broached the subject that had bugged him since Wednesday night.

"Who is he?"

"Hmm?" she asked without glancing his way.

"The guy who had you frowning when I came by on Wednesday, and now."

Her hazel eyes pierced him and narrowed. "How do you know what I'm thinking?"

"Because you have that look of a woman irritated by a man. Trust me, I know that look. I've seen it many times."

This made her laugh. She became less defensive,

turned her body and reached for a float. "Tell me about that."

"No way, Ms. Avoider," he replied. "We're talking about you right now."

He watched her nibble her plush lower lip and formulate an answer. "It's complicated," she said at last, her lips moist and swollen and looking so tasty that he wanted to nibble them himself. He ignored his twitching member.

Down, boy.

"Do you love him?" He refused to admit how much her answer mattered. She shook her head. "Then what's hard about it?"

"He's an ex who wants another chance. Our families are close. My dad likes him, and is the CFO of his father's company."

"Ah. That's complicated. Though I can understand the guy is probably kicking himself, trying to figure out how you got away."

"He'd be better served learning how not to be a jerk."

"Ha! Ready to get out of the water?"

"And do what?" She looked at him with suggestive eyes.

"Definitely that," he said with a knowing smile as he hoisted himself from the pool. "But later, after I run something past you."

Lauren floated over to the steps and climbed out, or tried to, as she tested putting weight on her ankle. He watched for a while just to drink in all that beauty as she slowly rose up from the pool like a nymph, water cascading off her hair, down her back and the long legs that had gripped him in the heat of passion. He saw her wince and went into action, closing the distance between them in two strides and lifting her out of the water as though she were made of glass.

"Hey, I can walk!"

"You can hop. There's a difference."

"Ha! Put me down, smart-ass."

He did, but ran his hands down her back and squeezed her butt, enjoying a juicy kiss before letting her go. She reached for the sarong made of bold animal print fabric that lay across a lounge chair and tied it around her hips. He took a towel from a nearby table, ran it over his hair and draped it across his shoulders. They entered the two-story great room that framed the pool. The tile floor was cool beneath their bare feet. Lauren hobbled over to one of a matching set of bamboo chairs covered in a lavish, water-resistant silk and sank into the plush cushion. She placed her legs on the ottoman nearby. Christian sat across from her on the couch and eyed her thoughtfully.

"So…what's up? What do you want to talk about?"

He cocked his head to one side. "How would you like to work for CANN?"

"I already do."

"Not the foundation, the corporation."

"With you as my boss? No, thanks."

Said with such mock seriousness, Christian laughed out loud. "There could be benefits to sleeping with the boss, you know."

"Yes, and even bigger disadvantages."

"Are you speaking from experience?" he asked.

Her brow rose. "Are you?"

"I learned early on that the old cliché was true. Business and pleasure do not mix well. I also believe that there can be exceptions to every rule."

Lauren nodded, her eyes intent as she waited.

"When Dad named the corporation after us boys using the CANN acronym, he purposely stayed away from campaigns using the word. Too obvious, he felt, and a bit corny. But not long ago a guy you may have heard about used it fairly successfully in a presidential campaign—" he paused as Lauren smiled "—and there was something about how you used it in the social media campaign that made common phrases sound oddly refreshing. I think that approach might work for this launch."

Christian thought this revelation might shock Lauren. Her surprised expression proved that he'd been correct.

"You want me to work on the marketing for your trillion-dollar baby? A campaign to bring the rich, famous and in-famous running to these shores?"

"Yes."

She pursed her lips. "Why?"

"Because of what I've seen, on your website and the internet, and even more by what I feel. It takes time for me to build trust with people, and while I generally don't trust women, I trust you."

"Why don't you trust women?" she queried.

"I've been lied to."

Lauren gave him a look. "Join the world of relation-ships."

Christian's smile was bittersweet.

Her tone turned serious. "That bad, huh?"

"In the eyes of my then-eighteen-year-old self it was worse."

"Care to share details?" she asked.

Christian looked away from her then, and out toward the pool. "Someone tried to trap me into marriage by saying she was pregnant."

"And she wasn't?"

He shrugged. "If she was, she didn't have it. I guess I'll never know."

"Did you ever see her again after that?" He nodded. "When was the last time?"

"Wednesday night. It was Chloe, right after breaking up with her once and for all."

"Judging by her reaction to me, she has yet to get over it." She shot him a look. "Are you over her?"

"Totally." He stood and walked over to where she sat in the chair. "I'm also done with this conversation, and have a much better idea for how we can spend the rest of the day."

"Great! What's that?"

Christian held out his hands to help her up. "Remember the promises I made on the airplane, the ones that involved your getting wet?"

Lauren nodded, the sweet blush on her skin proof that clearly she remembered.

"Well…it's time to be a man of my word."

The next morning, Monday, Christian was awakened by a shard of sunlight piercing his left eyelid. He squinted and ran his arm across the sheets in search of soft skin. Instead his fingers encountered a pillow and a part of the bunched-up sheet on the empty side of the bed. He reached for his phone, opened one eye fully to read the time. It was early, just eight o'clock. Considering the horizontal cardio they'd engaged in for hours the previous night, it was much too early to get up. But the custom king-size was lonely without her, so he rolled out of bed, slipped on a pair of shorts and went in search of Lauren.

She was in the kitchen, barefoot except for the ankle brace, wearing the skimpy negligee he'd removed last night. He slid up behind her, squeezed her luscious booty before pulling her back against him and nuzzling her neck.

"Hey," she cooed, moving out of his grasp.

A subtle move, but Christian noticed. Last night she only moved toward him, not away.

"Was it something I said?" he asked lightly. "Morning breath?" He cupped his hand and blew into it.

"No, silly."

The teapot sounded. He watched Lauren pour the scalding water over a tea bag.

"Want some?"

"Sure, why not?"

He walked over to a bar chair and eased into it, content for the moment to watch Lauren looking all kinds of sexy in the domestic scene.

"Black or green?"

His eyes narrowed. "Definitely black."

She smiled, licked her lips. "You're talking about the tea, right?"

"I'm so *not* talking about the tea, but I'll have that black, too."

She fixed the tea and brought the mugs over to where he sat, along with lemons and agave she'd found in the fridge. For several seconds they sat side by side, the only sound that of silverware clanking against china, soft blows and tiny sips.

Whether a personal or professional matter, Christian believed in the direct approach. So he turned to Lauren, tucked a strand of hair behind her ear and allowed his fingers to linger in her gorgeous curls. "What's going on in there?"

"A lot of thinking."

"About?"

She glanced at him. "You. This. Everything between us—the attraction, the hot sex, the family dynamic with our mothers being friends, me working for Victoria... potentially working with you."

"So you're considering my offer."

"You made an offer?" she murmured. "I don't recall."

"I asked the question of whether you'd consider working with me, or more specifically, working on the CANN Island campaign." He caught her gaze. "Are you?"

"I'd be interested in working under contract. I'd rather do that than become an employee right now."

"That could happen."

She nodded. "Which is why I woke up thinking that while the fireworks we create in bed could probably be declared illegal in a few countries and several states…"

He ran his fingers up her arm and watched goose bumps pop up in their wake.

"Like that," she breathed, and moved her arm. "I think it's probably best for now that we go back to just being friends."

"No benefits?"

"Well, maybe every now and then," she murmured with a face that made him laugh. "Seriously, though. There's a lot happening stateside that I need to sort out, and that's what I need to focus on right now."

"The complicated ex?"

"The series of major events by the foundation over the next few months," she clarified. "It's a short contract, but I want to do my best. Hopefully the situation with…my personal issues…will require very little of my attention."

"Good. Because I'd like for us to work out the details of your proposed contract with CANN as soon as possible, and put you and that brilliant mind of yours right to work."

"Have you forgotten that I'm under contract with CANN Foundation?"

"Yes, but without the continued success of CANN In-

ternational, there is no foundation. Don't worry. I'll talk
to Mom. We'll work something out."

One of the hosts called and a short time later Christian
and Lauren were picked up and whisked away to have
lunch at the president's palace. He was led into another
meeting and as was often the case in Muslim countries,
only the men were invited. He not only felt bad but, considering the intricate role Lauren might play in the Island
brand, was a bit miffed that she'd been excluded. Later he
learned that one of the wives had taken her "shopping,"
a limited proposition, and to enjoy local cuisine—oven-
baked fish, chapati, *mukbassa*—at Mukbassa Central
Chez Youssouf.

On Tuesday, once business was done for the day, he
and Lauren joined a French businessman and his wife
for a turn in the canal in a glass-bottom boat. They were
taken to where the magic of the coral reefs below the
water was clear and brilliant to the naked eye without
having to go underwater. They went farther out and
watched dolphins play.

The following afternoon they left Djibouti and, remembering Lauren's suggestion to be "just friends" once
stateside, took full advantage of their remaining time together. They'd barely reached cruising altitude before he
pulled her into the jet's swanky bedroom and initiated a
different kind of high, one where he thrusted, plunged
and branded her insides. Lauren matched his enthusiasm
and gave as good as she got. He rewarded her efforts with
a final push that took her over the edge and into the status as a climax-carrying member of the mile-high club.

An hour before landing in Italy, an impromptu side
trip before heading home, they showered and dressed
and returned to the main cabin. Lauren read a magazine,
leaving Christian to pick at his dinner and be alone with

his thoughts. He replayed what Lauren had said in Djibouti about why their sexual escapades needed to end and found irony in how closely her reasoning actually matched his own. At least it had when it came to other women. But with Lauren, all of that logic seemed to fly out the window. He didn't want what started last week to be over, and the fact that she worked with his mother? Well, at the moment, he just didn't give a damn.

Fifteen

Lauren felt like a jet-setter. On Wednesday, she and Christian had left Djibouti for Rome. When asked why they were going there, Christian had answered, his tone sincere, "I'm hungry and in the mood for Italian." They'd eaten at the only restaurant in the eternal city with three Michelin stars, enjoying delicacies Lauren had never imagined, like rabbit tortellini with carrot and chamomile, white asparagus with seaweed pesto, and fillet of John Dory with almond cream and lemon shrimp. The view was glorious and afterward they'd toured the famous ruins, thrown coins in the Trevi Fountain, and walked off dessert by testing out the strength of both the bionic brace and her ankle by climbing a few of the Spanish Steps.

Since Italy was one of the world's most romantic countries, she was glad her "no sex with Christian" rule was not yet in effect, and that she'd agreed that there could be occasional benefits to their friendship. She couldn't picture herself being here, especially with a hunk like the eldest Breedlove boy, and not making love.

Earlier today they'd left for Las Vegas. The whirlwind trip had left her exhausted, and she awoke to find her head on Christian's shoulder, his arm comfortably around her. She jerked upright and looked around. The plane was about to land.

"Sorry, I didn't mean to use your shoulder for a pillow."

"Baby, you can use any part of me anytime you want to."

"Come on now. We talked about that already. What happened in Djibouti is going to stay in Djibouti, right?"

"What about what happened over the Atlantic Ocean and in Rome?" Lauren made a face. "Is that really what you want?"

"No, but I think it's best."

Christian exhaled roughly. "Being that you work for my mother, you're probably right."

"So you agree with me?"

"I wouldn't go that far," he replied.

"Working for Victoria is one reason, but not the only one."

He reached out and gently tilted her face toward his. "You sure it isn't the ex?"

"It's everything we've already discussed. Let's leave it at that, okay?"

"If that's what you want." Christian's phone rang. "Excuse me."

Lauren was grateful for the interruption even as she reached for her own phone, rarely used while in Africa. She'd become more and more uncomfortable with Christian's probing questions about Ed. The fewer people who knew about the "arranged marriage" that her father desired, the better.

She turned on her phone and while it powered up looked out the window at the familiar Las Vegas skyline, the hotels along the Strip, CANN the most grandiose—a gleaming mass of steel and glass jutting into the sky—and was surprised to feel as though she were coming home. Although she'd only been in Vegas a short time, she already felt like she belonged there, more so than she'd felt after years on the East Coast.

That revelation was much too complicated to mentally process, because she knew that the feeling had everything to do with the man beside her. The man she could see herself easily falling in love with, and also the last man she should date. At least now, while her life was in such turmoil.

The plane touched down just after noon on the West Coast. She said goodbye to the crew and the pilot while Christian was preoccupied, and then began checking a slew of text messages and noting missed calls. Was there something wrong? Her brow furrowed as he assisted her down the stairs.

"Back to the real world," he said.

"Yep." She continued scrolling her phone.

"Is everything okay?"

"I hope so."

They reached Christian's car. During the short ride to the guesthouse she was quiet, listening to messages left by several people, including her friend Avery and her mom. He pulled into the drive, put the car in Park and jumped out to get her luggage from the trunk. He wheeled it up to the door and after she'd entered the code, rolled them inside.

She turned to him with a genuine smile. "Thank you."

"Where do you want them?" he asked.

"Here is fine," she replied, with a wave across the living room area.

"Sure you don't want them in your bedroom?"

She shrugged. "I guess that would be better."

"Sure you don't want to join me in the bedroom?"

"Stop it, Christian. We've already had that discussion, the outcome of which does not involve bedrooms."

"You can't knock a brother for trying."

"No, but I can knock a brother *out* for making the attempt."

They laughed. He pulled her into his arms. "I forgot, the wildcat."

"No, a bear."

"Dangerous either way." After a tender squeeze, he released her. "Thank you for joining me in Djibouti. Your presence made the trip infinitely more pleasurable, and not just physically. Your beauty is only outshone by your intelligence."

She rolled her eyes.

"This isn't bullshit," he said. "I'm serious. You're an amazing woman and I'm lucky… CANN International is lucky to have you on our team. So I'll say it again. Thank you…for everything."

His words were so heartfelt and tender, they almost drew tears. Lauren covered the emotion by reaching for the crutch and heading toward the door.

"You're very welcome, Mr. Breedlove," she said as she opened it for him to walk through. "The pleasure was totally and completely mine, but from now on, it's back to work."

Lauren closed the door and leaned against it, willing herself not to cry at what could never be. The missed text messages and phone calls she'd read upon landing were the sobering reminder needed to snap back to reality and get a handle on what was going on. She walked into the bedroom, tapped the phone's screen and called her mom. The familiar message of Faye not being available encouraged her to leave a message at the sound of the beep. She didn't. Instead she ended the call and scrolled to Avery's number. She put the call on speaker and peeled off her clothes, donning a short silk robe when Avery answered.

"It's about time!"

Lauren laughed. "I just got home."

"How dare you send me a text about exotic travels and private planes and then be unavailable for the next week!"

"I guess I should have waited."

"No, then I would have been angry that you'd left me out. But I'm here now. Tell me everything!"

Lauren gave a condensed recap of her trip to Djibouti. "I can honestly say I've never felt so happy, yet completely conflicted at the same time."

A flood of emotions poured through Lauren, making her mind roil and her heart ache. But obsessing over what it all meant would have to wait, she realized, checking the face of her cell phone as the text indicator pinged.

"Avery, listen, I've got to go."

"You've got to be kidding!"

"I'll call you later, promise."

Lauren meant every word. She was sure that later she'd need someone to talk to. She tapped her cell phone's face again and read the text her mom had sent. The second one after explaining she couldn't talk because she was at the library doing research. She read it again, slowly, mouthing the incredible words.

Honey, your dad is in Vegas. And Ed is with him.

And just like that, the dream of a week she'd just spent with Christian crashed into the nightmare that she'd briefly escaped. Lauren sat stunned. What were they doing here? There was only one way to find out. She called her dad's cell phone. Paul must have been sitting right by it. He picked up on the first ring.

She was exhausted from all the travel and all the love-making and belatedly realized that maybe she should have waited to make the call. But there was no getting around it. A face-to-face showdown with both Dad and Ed was inevitable.

"Lauren, where are you?"

"Dad, why are you here?" She felt her question was the one that mattered. "And why is Ed with you?" The answer to that mattered even more.

"Lorrie, we need to talk."

No, not the term of endearment he'd used since she was a child, the only one allowed to call her by that name. It came out in the rush of a relieved breath, and wafted through the phone to her heart, gripping it gently.

She tapped the speaker button, sat on the edge of her bed. "Dad…"

"I have been worried sick about you."

"Why?"

"First you take a job without my knowing about it, then flee the East Coast with barely a goodbye. Now I hear you're traveling to God only knows where with that Breedlove character, a playboy from what I hear, who seems to go through women the way an omelet maker goes through eggs. This type of behavior is so unlike you. You've never acted this way before."

"I've never felt pressured into marriage before!" The words, delivered with missile-like precision, were regretted within syllables of their leaving her mouth. But they were true, and while she'd never want to hurt her father, his actions had caused her heart to bleed.

"Lorrie, I need to see you. Tonight."

"I'll talk to you, but not him."

A long silence and then, "All right. Should I come to you?"

"No. I'll come to you. Where are you staying?"

"The CANN."

Of course. "What room?" He told her. "Okay, fine. I'll be there in an hour. And I mean it, Daddy. You'd better be alone."

An hour later she pulled into the valet area. This was the first instance she'd entered through the main lobby entrance. She was struck by its vast grandeur and elegant style. At once modern and classic, with Victoria's imprint everywhere.

She reached the elevator and pushed the button, trying to forget why she was here. Each time she remembered her heartbeat quickened, and a sickening knot began to form in her gut. Who knew? Maybe this visit was about the business project between Ed and her dad and had nothing to do with this arranged marriage nonsense. That thought brought a good feeling, so much so that when she reached the fourteenth floor and headed toward the room number her father had given, she allowed herself to get just a little excited about the upcoming visit. She was going to see her dad!

Lauren arrived at the room and announced her presence with a rhythmic *rat-ta-tat-tat*. The door opened and there stood Paul Hart, eyes bright, mouth taut, a little slimmer than she remembered.

"Hi, Dad." She stepped into the room and into his embrace, her eyes misting unexpectedly at the familiar woodsy fragrance of his cologne. She held him at arm's length and looked him over. "Have you lost weight?"

"Perhaps a pound or two," he said. He smiled and crinkles appeared at the sides of his eyes. He stepped back and eyed the blinged-out sock London had given her. "Faye told me about your ankle. How is it?"

"Better every day."

"A horse threw you, correct?"

"Yes. She got spooked by a snake and I couldn't hang on. First time I'd handled reins in years."

"I remember how you used to love it, though. You learned on Robert's old nag, remember?"

Lauren thought about the ramshackle farm in Georgia, the one owned by her dad and her uncle Robert's father. The one that left the family's hands when Robert ran into financial problems and her father refused to bail him out. Lauren was saddened at losing the family land but couldn't blame her father. He'd bailed out Uncle Robert a lot.

"You look beautiful, Lorrie, though a little tired around the eyes. Are you being overworked?"

"I'm fine." With a limp barely noticeable, she took in the room as she walked over to the sitting area by the window—two high-backed chairs framing a round metal table covered with glass. The king-size bed looked grand and imposing, its brass-studded headboard with tufted black fabric covering a mattress that seemed to promise a heavenly night's sleep. It was a comfort her hardworking father deserved yet one that, given his sensible spending, surprised her. This single king-size room went for an average of two thousand dollars a night.

"I can understand why you chose the CANN but given the room rates, I'm surprised that you did."

"The company's paying for it, honey. My money doesn't stretch this far."

"So this *is* a business trip."

"Yes and no." Paul reached for a tumbler on a mini-bar counter Lauren just realized was there. She frowned slightly as he came over and sat down. Her father enjoyed a good, neat scotch and cigar as well as the next guy but usually only once in a while, after dinner, late at night. That it was midday and no food had been served caused a slight nervous flutter to return to her stomach.

"Dad, why are you here?"

"As I said before, we need to talk."

"What is so important that couldn't be discussed by phone?"

"Your future and making sure the choices you make are the right ones. When Faye told me you'd left the country with that notorious playboy, well, I knew you weren't thinking clearly."

"I'm a big girl, Daddy, a grown woman in fact. My mind is clear. I can take care of myself."

"Men like Breedlove are dangerous. You need someone sensible and grounded, who'll keep you safe in a loving home."

"And you think that's Ed?" Lauren snorted.

"Yes, I think that's Ed. And before you use my predicament as an excuse, this is not just about the money I owe. Over the past several months, I've had time to make my own observations. Ed is pragmatic and responsible, and he has loved you for a very long time. He believes that you two can be a power couple, that together our families can create a dynasty of generational wealth. Now, I don't know what happened years ago when you dated, but I think he's deserving of another chance."

"Dad, you've never cared one iota about who I've dated," she scoffed. "How can I not assume that your taking a loan from Ed has something to do with this new glowing view of him?"

"That I've never cared is not true. I've always been concerned, you just didn't know it. Ask your mother. She'll tell you. A secure future for my girls is all I've ever wanted. Thomas is a good man. Perfect for Renee."

She suppressed the urge to roll her eyes. "And you think Ed is perfect for me."

"Ed has become like a son to me. The one I've always wanted."

"Then I suggest you work something out with his dad, some kind of bilateral adoption so that he can join the family. An annoying older brother? Now that I can imagine. But a power couple, or any couple, Dad, that's not going to happen. When it comes to Ed Miller I couldn't be less interested. I am not going to date him. I am not going to marry him. There is nothing you can say that will make me change my mind."

A slight *click*, and then movement caught the corner of Lauren's eye. Ed was coming toward them, obviously from an adjoining room.

"I think there is something that might sway you, dear," he said with a sickening smile. "Paul, do you want to tell her? Or should I?"

Sixteen

Christian knew there were several issues that required his attention that day but decided to work from home. He reached for the vibrating phone on his desk, looked at the number and sighed. Evidently the word had gotten out about Lauren joining him in Africa. He hadn't told her during their trip, but his phones had been blowing up with calls from half a dozen other women he'd casually dated in the past. Females who'd agreed to no-strings-attached friendships but had secretly hoped they might become Mrs. B.

That his private life hadn't remained private was extremely annoying. When it came to promoting the business, Christian lived for the camera, searched out chances for positive PR. Which made him even more guarded when it came to his private life. The less anyone outside of his family knew, the better.

No doubt Chloe was behind the leak that could only

have led to rampant gossip. She always managed to know his business. If Christian ever discovered her source, that person would be fired immediately.

He leaned against the back of his chair, locked his fingers behind his head and turned to stare out the window at the peacocks dotting his backyard. He watched a pair of peahens walk by the three peacocks he'd personally chosen from a breeder in California. Similar to their human counterparts, when females were about, the cocks immediately began strutting their stuff, spreading their plumage in all its glory.

Christian smiled as the peahens continued across the yard to a fountain designed to not only provide them continuous water but to power an Old West water wheel churning into a koi pond. The age-old dance of court and conquer continued. The game had changed, he mused, thinking of the calls he'd ignored. These days, it was sometimes the woman shaking her tail feathers in hopes of attracting the man.

His thoughts drifted to the past couple years and the types of women he'd dated. And the years before that when he'd been the peacock, when his trust had been tested and broken.

Chloe. Who'd claimed to be pregnant, and wasn't. Pamela, who'd been snapped by a tabloid wearing a huge diamond ring and had hinted it was an engagement ring from Christian. It wasn't, and the lie led to the breakup with Erica, a Bahamian beauty, who at that time he thought was the love of his life. Natalie, who'd filed a felonious police report in an attempt to extort five million dollars from his family.

That nonsense with Natalie was the final straw that caused Christian to declare he'd never trust a woman again. Moreover, it had propelled him to set very clear boundaries with the women he dated, and brought on the need for confidentiality and nondisclosure agreements and women being vetted before they could enter his world.

His phone vibrated again. He didn't want to answer the call but pulled himself away from the window and crossed to the desk. Lauren. He smiled. The peahen who'd made him once again want to stick out his chest and spread his feathers, the one who not once had made him think about contracts and vetting.

A while back he'd wondered what it was about her that he found so intriguing. In this moment the answer came clearly: Lauren wanted nothing from him. He pressed the speaker button and answered the call.

"Hey, beautiful."

"Hey, hubby."

Her voice was sexy, seductive, made his manhood throb and reminded him of...wait. Did she say hubby?

"Sorry to bother you. I know you're working. But I'm here with my dad and he doesn't believe we got married."

Christian pulled the phone away from his ear and rechecked the name. Yes, it was the number he'd locked in the night of the fashion show, with a picture he'd snapped of Lauren lounging at his home in Djibouti, smiling from the screen. To say he was confused was an understatement. Was she trying to play a joke?

"Ed is here, too." *Ed? A former boyfriend?* "Ed Miller, my ex, the one I told you about in Djibouti."

The words made Christian's heart squeeze, along with the sound of subtle panic in Lauren's voice. It was high and bright and overly girlie, not the low, sometimes monotone quality he'd grown to love.

And she'd called him hubby. Said they'd gotten married. Something was going on. But what?

"Where are you?"

"At the ho—"

"Lauren?" He looked at the screen. It was black. The call had dropped. Or had it been disconnected? Was she okay? Why had her father come to town and brought her ex with him? His mind reeling with all the possible implications, he impatiently hit redial. The call rang and rang and finally went to voice mail. He hung up and tried again. Same thing. He called the hotel.

"Thank you for calling CANN, America's first seven-star hotel. My name is Zena. How may I help make your day amazing?"

"Zena, this is Chris Breedlove. I need to be connected to…" In this moment he realized he didn't know the name of Lauren's dad. "To a Mr. Hart."

There was a long pause. "His first name, please?"

"I don't know."

"I'm sorry, but I'll need his entire name to connect the call. We can't provide any information on our guests."

"Did you hear me? This is Chris Breedlove. As in the president of the hotel that employs you. As in your boss."

"I'm really so sorry, but how do I know this is you? We have very strict policies regarding the privacy of our—"

Cursing under his breath, Christian hung up the phone. It may have been the first time in his life he was pissed at someone for explicitly following the rules and being great at their job. And why hadn't Lauren called him back? Suddenly more concerned for her welfare than aggravated at the abrupt disconnection, or her call, he left his office and headed toward the hallway that led to his garage. He paused just briefly in front of the rack of keys beside the door, grabbed the one to his sports Lexus coupe and pushed the button to open the third garage door.

Seconds after he'd backed out of the space and headed down the long driveway, his Bluetooth announced a call. He hoped it was Lauren. It wasn't.

"Mom, has Lauren called you?"

"I'm well, son, thanks for asking. Good afternoon to you, too!"

"Sorry, but I don't have time for formalities right now. I just got a weird call from Lauren. She might be in trouble."

"What was weird about it?"

"For starters she lied to her father, told him that we got married in Djibouti!"

"Oh, dear."

"I told her about how Chloe tried to trap me and here she goes and does the same thing!"

"Lauren isn't manipulative like Chloe, honey. For her to do what she did, there had to be a very good reason. Something concerning her safety, or that of someone she loves."

"Do you know something?" he demanded.

"I probably have an idea."

"Well?" A frustrated hand ran through his tightly curled coils as he navigated the roadway. "Do you want to let me in on it? Wait, did you already know about this?"

"About her saying you two were married? Of course not. I do know she left the East Coast to get away from an annoying, determined ex, the one who is probably at the hotel right now. If that's true, then I'm sure she had a very good reason to do what she did, and an explanation that will make everything make sense. For her to take such drastic action, her back had to be against the wall. Just let her explain, okay?"

Christian had heard enough. He shifted gears and gave the sporty luxury vehicle the chance to live up to its claim of zero to sixty in seconds. Victoria wouldn't tell him what was happening. Christian didn't care. All he knew was that Lauren had better do the right thing. He couldn't get to the hotel fast enough.

Seventeen

The unexpected, insistent knock at the door caused all three in the room to jump. Conversation ceased mid-sentence as Lauren, Paul and Ed looked toward the door. Lauren's first thought was that someone had called security. Their talking had grown heated, and voices were raised. Perhaps, like her, a guest in one of the adjoining rooms had heard enough.

After sharing a brief look with her father, Ed walked to the door. He peered out the peephole.

"Who is it?" Paul asked.

"I don't know," Ed said, still looking.

"Security?"

Lauren's dad had voiced her thought.

"I don't think so," was Ed's curt reply.

Another knock came. It was louder this time, as though done with the meaty part of the hand and not with the knuckles.

"Lauren," the person outside of the room said. "I know you're in there. Open the door."

Christian!

She moved toward the door.

Ed spun around with his arm out. "Stay back."

"Open the door," Lauren said, feeling as though Christian were the cavalry come to save her. "Let him in!"

Another banging from the other side of the wood. "I'm giving you three seconds to open this door. Do it, or I will."

With one final glare, Ed opened the door. "Who are you?" he demanded. "And what do you want?"

Two seconds after the door to the hotel suite opened, Lauren knew what a knight in shining armor looked like. Christian took the cliché of tall, dark and handsome to a whole other level, and with his shoulders squared, eyes darkened with fury and his panther-like movements, he looked like a superhero. He pushed past Ed, who turned as if to attack him from behind.

"Don't even think about it." Delivered in a voice that was deadly quiet as the person behind it, Adam stepped through the door.

"Who are you?" Paul demanded. "What are you doing in my room?"

"Not quite the way I envisioned meeting my father-in-law," Christian drawled as he crossed the room, reached Lauren and slid a possessive arm around her waist. "But Mr. Hart—I assume you are Mr. Hart—I've come to collect my wife."

Paul's gaze shifted from Christian to Lauren. Her heart broke at the look of hurt in his eyes, and something else that seconds later she realized was abject fear.

"Do you want to stay here?" Christian asked her.

"No," she replied softly, as the gravity of the situation and of her knee-jerk declaration began to sink in.

She moved toward her father. "Come with me, Daddy, so we can talk."

"You'd better take her up on it," Ed snarled. "It will be one of the last times you'll get a chance to do it without a sheet of Plexiglas between you."

Christian turned to Ed. "Is that a threat?"

"What's it to you? Mind your business. As for you—" Ed pointed an accusatory finger at Lauren "—know that whatever happens to Paul from now on lands squarely on your shoulders. Your father is getting ready to take a fall and you're the one to blame."

"Not if Gerald has anything to say about it. Unlike you, your dad is an upstanding man with character and integrity. He'll give Dad time to pay back what he owes. So save your threats for someone they'll scare."

"Do you think this is about money? No, it's about you. And if this marriage actually happened, you'll regret it, mark my words. There's more than one way to bring a man down. And his entire family along with him."

"That's enough." Two words delivered with such quiet authority that the room quieted in an instant. Christian stared at Ed for several heated seconds before speaking to Lauren.

"Sweetheart, why don't we give your father some time alone? I think everyone could use a break, a chance to calm down and…" Lauren felt his body stiffen as he turned to her ex. "A chance for you to get your things and get the hell out of my hotel."

Christian turned to Adam. "Can you handle that for me, baby bro?"

"Wait a damn minute," Ed snarled, clearly unaccustomed to being told what to do. "I'm a paying guest and this is a public space. You can't throw me out."

Christian took a step toward Ed. Adam blocked his

path. "Take care of Lauren, brother." He slid his eyes toward Ed with quiet determination. "I've got this."

"Dad..." Lauren began, but Christian's grip suggested she had one choice, and that was to go with him.

"Your dad will be fine, Lauren," Adam said. "You have my word."

Lauren hugged her father. "Everything will work out," she whispered, having no idea given what she'd heard how that could be true. She reached for her purse without so much as a glance at Ed.

"This isn't over," he told her.

"It's over," Christian said.

He opened the door and led Lauren out of the hotel room without looking back.

"I can explain everything," Lauren whispered, mere seconds into the hallway.

From Christian, not a word, but the hold on her arm relaxed.

"I'm sorry," she offered.

His silence was loud.

They reached the elevator. He pushed the up button.

"Where are we going?" Lauren asked.

The elevator arrived. Christian pulled out a card and slid it into the slot. A panel opened, revealing six unmarked buttons. He pushed the top button on the right. Pulled out his card. The panel closed. He leaned against the elevator wall and stared straight ahead.

"Are you going to say anything?"

A sigh underscored his annoyance. "We're going where total and complete privacy is guaranteed. Once there, the only one who will be talking is you."

The suite they entered was beyond luxurious. The first thing Lauren noticed was the pool on the balcony more than a hundred feet in the air. She knew this wasn't the day for a guided tour, though. As soon as the door closed, Christian laid into her.

"Speak."

Lauren was immediately affronted but calmed herself down. He'd been blindsided by her the way she'd been bushwhacked by her father. He had a right to be angry and right now, she did not.

"Ed is blackmailing my dad."

She expected a response. When it didn't happen, she looked up. Christian stood waiting, arms crossed, clearly wondering what Ed and her father's issues had to do with him and marriage.

"It's a personal situation involving my father. What's happening between him and Ed is not my problem, or secret to share. To do so could get my dad in trouble. I know it sounds crazy and I want to, but I can't."

"You have no choice. Obviously your father coming here made his problem yours, one that caused you to lie and say we were married. Which now makes me involved in whatever's happening and that, darling, gives me a right to know all."

Lauren watched Christian cross the room and take a seat, as if to underscore the fact that without some type of answers they weren't going anywhere.

"You're right." She took a deep breath and joined him on the couch. "First of all, I'm so sorry for involving you. I'm not prone to lying and obviously don't do it very well, especially when in a state of shock. Finding out that my dad was here was enough of a surprise, but learning that Ed was with him only added to my angst."

"While this is all very interesting, sweetheart, would you mind cutting to the chase?"

"Okay…fine." Clenching her hands together on her

lap, she finally blurted, "I thought Dad borrowed money from Ed. He didn't. He embezzled from the company and Ed found out. Ed threatened to file criminal charges on Dad unless he and I got married."

"And you thought to get out of marrying Ed by saying you were already married to me."

"The words jumped out before I could catch them. I didn't have time to think about the repercussions or you even finding out. It was just so I could buy enough time to help my father pay back what he owes Ed. But he didn't believe me so I was forced to call you and prove it was true."

"To prove that your lie was the truth."

Christian's brow furrowed. Even in her dismay Lauren couldn't help notice that she'd never seen a finer scowl.

"Basically."

"Why did your dad steal from the company?"

"That was the hard part of what I learned, the piece of the puzzle Dad kept from everyone, even my mom." Lauren paused, her heart breaking with the thought of how her proud father would never want anyone to know of the depths gone to because of his financial plight.

"He was deeply in debt and never told us, had taken out a huge bank loan with their beautiful, forever dream home as collateral. He borrowed the money to repay that loan."

"He embezzled company funds to pay off a loan?"

"Yes, one that a friend at the bank set up to be repaid over a longer time than was usually allowed. That friend left. His replacement demanded the repayment be made immediately and in full. Dad is one of the most honest, upstanding and loyal men I've ever known. He fully intended to put back what he borrowed without anyone knowing what happened."

"But Ed found out," Christian surmised.

"Unfortunately, yes, which means Gerald, Ed's father who not only owns the company but is my dad's good friend, could also know the truth if Ed carried out the threat to tell him. Or worse, to call the police. Having Gerald think less of him would kill my father, and having the embezzlement made public would be like a tombstone on the grave. His name and reputation mean everything."

"How can a father use his own daughter as a pawn in a business deal?"

"I'm sure Dad didn't see it that way, at least not at first. Ed can be convincing. He had my father thinking that his intentions toward me were honorable. His true nature and threats of blackmail came only after I refused to go along with the plan.

"For the past few years it's been one blow after another, with my father treading water while trying to right a sinking ship. The moment Ed decided to check those books, his luck ran out."

"How much money are we talking?"

"Well into six figures. Enough to make what my father did a felony that, if Ed goes through with his threat, could get Dad locked up for a very long time."

"So Ed threatened to have your father charged if he couldn't have you. Sounds like a man obsessed, and after our trip to Africa, I can understand why."

The sudden tenderness in Christian's voice made Lauren's eyes misty and produced a slight smile. "I appreciate your saying that but trust me, the only person Ed is obsessed with is himself. He's used to getting what he wants and can't handle rejection."

"Ah, so you rejected him."

"Not fast enough," she confessed. "As you may have

guessed, he's the ex I've mentioned several times when we've talked about dating."

"I did. The ex who now wants you back."

"The ex who wants to save face. Apparently he found another girl like I'd been, young, naive, and told everyone they'd be married. When their relationship ended, he needed another bride. That's when he tried to get back with me. My answer was no, unequivocally.

"His anger at the rejection and potential embarrassment turned into obsession. I had no idea he harbored these feelings, though, not until my dad did what he did and Ed felt he finally had a way to make me obey him. He's obsessed, but he doesn't love me. He wants to have his way. He wants control."

"That's why he's trying to force you into marriage, to keep your dad out of jail."

"Yes." Lauren turned toward Christian, her eyes angry, determined. "But I will not be manipulated. I just need time to figure out a solution. That's what I was thinking when I did what I did."

"But why me, though? You could have said you married anybody, even made up a name."

"I told you why. It was a reflex. I didn't have time to think."

Christian stood and walked over to the window. Lauren could only imagine how he felt. She'd given him a lot to process, and that while still being in shock herself.

Christian began speaking, still gazing out the window. All traces of tenderness were gone. "If what you said is true, it's a horrible story."

"What do you mean, if?"

He turned around. "I think you know the meaning of that word. And you know I've been lied to before."

"You think I'm lying, that I've made all of this up?"

Lauren got up and walked toward him, sure that he had to be speaking in jest. One look at his face, however, and she knew he was as serious as a brain surgeon in the operating room.

"Women have made up more for less."

Lauren was speechless. Not that it mattered, as Christian had much more to say.

"You show up suddenly and out of nowhere to work for my mother and within what, days, are in my bed."

"With a sprained ankle!"

"You push your way," he continued, voice raised, "into the company and the next thing you know you're heading to Africa on a private plane."

"You came to me with the idea of traveling to Africa."

"Only after my mother campaigned on your behalf."

"And I somehow manipulated that? I somehow put her up to having me take a trip I knew nothing about?" She shot daggers at him. "I didn't invite myself to Africa. You asked that I join you. And now that's my fault? Are you *kidding* me right now?"

"Do I look like I'm joking? My life is not a game, but I've been in it long enough to know that people will go to all sorts of lengths to get what they want, and I believe anybody is capable of doing anything."

Lauren was beyond livid. She couldn't think, could barely feel. Did he know how hard it had been to share the shame of her father? How he was being blackmailed and her back was against the wall?

"Somehow, this just got twisted. The only way that could have happened is for you not to have understood what I said."

"Oh, I understood you," he bit out.

"So you don't believe me? Is that it?"

Christian spun away from the window and stalked toward the door. "I don't know what to believe, but I know this. If one word about this fake marriage gets made public, you're going to have much bigger problems than you do right now."

Eighteen

Lauren hadn't thought it possible to get angrier than she already was when Christian arrived in her father's room. But after their private conversation? She was surprised flames hadn't burst from her head. She could understand his being upset. She'd lied about their relationship, put him on the spot and involved him in a family matter much messier than she'd thought. But to think she'd done it on purpose? That there may have been an ulterior motive all along? What a blatant show of unmitigated gall!

Really? You lied to a man and he called you on it. And you're mad at him?

Lauren shrugged the devil off her shoulder and gripped the wheel. She hadn't planned to involve Christian in her drama. It had just happened. A small but necessary fabrication that would never be uttered outside of that hotel room. She hadn't had time to contemplate Christian's reaction, but couldn't have imagined he'd go ballistic.

All she wanted, and what she'd planned to tell him before the proverbial feces had hit the fan, was for Ed to think she was unavailable just long enough for her to sort everything out. She only thought to pretend she was married, and then only when she felt backed into the corner by the man she loved most in the entire world. A man who embezzled from his company, she thought, and the realization made her die just a little.

And then another thought rushed to the surface, one she had previously refused to consider no matter what, but now topped her very limited list of options. Marrying Ed would keep her dad out of prison.

Which brought her to the true crux of the matter—could she turn her back on her father and watch him go to jail when she had the power to keep him out?

One thing was for sure. She could not, would not, remain in Nevada. Whatever happened with her dad and however she helped him navigate the future, it would be far away from the man who thought her a liar, a manipulator and a conniving fraud.

By the time she reached Breedlove and the estate, Lauren had formulated a foolproof plan. She tapped her Bluetooth to call Victoria. She wanted to be packed and out of there by morning. There wasn't a second to lose.

"Lauren, how are you? Is everything okay?"

"I've been better. Are you busy? Something's come up and I need to speak with you. Can I come by?"

"Certainly. Bypass the circular drive and come around back when you get here. Nicholas and I are enjoying drinks by the pool."

"Okay, but can we speak privately?"

"Of course."

She reached the estate and instead of turning left toward her guesthouse after being waved through by the guard, turned in the direction of the family mansion. A profusion of color from the tall trees that lined the drive bathed Lauren's chilled body in their majestic warmth. The peacocks that roamed the estate and that she had come to love strutted around proudly, roaming over the expansive front lawn. The pond stocked with fresh fish glimmered in the distance, and beyond it the orchard of pomegranate, apple, fig and plum trees dotted the countryside in perfect alignment. The estate was breathtaking, a veritable paradise. Lauren acknowledged a feeling of sadness. She was going to miss this place.

She drove past the circular drive as Victoria had instructed and followed it around the house and to a guest parking lot across from a side entrance, hidden from view by a wraparound fence, a gate and trees. She reached for her purse. Her determination faltered a bit, but she had to see this through. Taking a deep, energizing breath, she exited the car and hurried over to the backyard as fast as she could manage with her still-healing ankle, now throbbing from overuse.

Nicholas and Victoria were seated in one of several outdoor living spaces. Lauren hadn't seen this one before. Even in her anger, she could see the beauty showing through. Stone tile in deep, rich colors flowed from the back of the house to the pergola anchoring the far side patio. The pergola held intimate seating, glass-top tables and a fireplace. Next to it was an outdoor kitchen and to the right an infinity pool. She approached Christian's parents with a tentative smile. His father, Nicholas, debonair and incredibly handsome at fifty-five, stood as she approached.

"Hello, Lauren."

"Hello, Nicholas."

Something about his baritone voice and the fatherly way he hugged her almost caused Lauren to burst into tears. But she dug her nails into her palm and clamped down the emotion. She was in a predicament at least partly of her own creation, and while breaking down and losing it would be totally understandable, she donned her big-girl panties, squared her shoulders and leaned down to give Victoria a hug.

"Hi, Victoria."

"I know you want to have girl talk," Nicholas said to Lauren. "But I spoke with Christian on his way back from Djibouti. He told me about you possibly coming on board for the CANN Island project and drawing up a contract to keep you with us for a while. Given how successful you were with the fashion fund-raiser, I'm extremely excited about that."

Lauren sat down as Nicholas walked away, glad he hadn't waited for the response informing him that a contract between her and Christian would never happen. Nor would anything else. Before the sadness in her belly could rise to her throat, she cleared it and began speaking.

"Victoria, something has come up and I want my contract terminated. Wait." She held up a hand. "Before you think this is déjà vu, please let me explain."

She provided a recap of what happened with Ed, with her dad and with Christian.

"In retrospect, *terminated* wasn't the right word. The day has been crazy and I can't think straight. I should have said modified.

"I will still do everything required in the agreement, but I'll do it from Maryland. Frankie and I have a great working relationship. He's talented and capable, and I trust him completely to carry out every detail. I can also fly in as the events approach and stay for several days until they're completed. I'm willing to do that at my own expense."

Victoria was quiet for a long moment. "First of all, darling, I'm terribly sorry for what you're going through. It's horrific, and criminal, and I think you should fight to not be dragged down in the mud. But running away is rarely a good answer." She reached out and squeezed Lauren's hand. "You ran here, right? And trouble followed. It is difficult but necessary to separate personal from business. For that reason I will not allow the agreement to be voided. This may sound harsh, Lauren, and I truly do empathize very much with your situation. But I will not aid in you abandoning your responsibilities, the foundation or me. The agreement must be honored."

Christian pulled into the circular drive but instead of going through the front door he walked around the back-yard outdoor space where his mom often worked. He was mildly surprised to see Lauren's car there, extremely angry at the version of events that she was probably spinning to try to get Victoria on her side. He bounded out of the car and up to the door, took a breath to try to compose himself before walking inside. The effort was only partly successful. Fortunately it took him several minutes to find the two women. By the time he'd discovered them seated on a marble bench among vibrant exotic flowers and gurgling fountains, he'd gained control of his anger.

Lauren, apparently, had not.

One look at Christian and she rose from the bench, barely concealing what to Christian appeared to be an expression of disgust. "Victoria, I appreciate everything you've done for me. But I ask that you reconsider your decision and call Frankie."

"Seriously?" Christian called out after her. "You fabricate a marriage and then act like I'm the bad guy?"

Lauren wheeled around. "No, you're the guy who called me a liar!"

"Oh, my bad. I thought someone told her daddy that I was the husband, the man she'd married while in Djibouti."

"You know what I mean," she spat through gritted teeth, walking back to him with a finger aimed at his chest. "Yes, I lied and said I was married. I also told you why. I felt I had no choice! I laid all my cards out on the table, shared confidentialities because you'd accept nothing less, and what do I get back? Your cynicism and disbelief, your haughty, self-absorbed accusations. On the worst night of my life I learn that you've been living with the delusional premise that I've hoodwinked your mom, moved across the country and flipped my world upside down all because of you."

Her next step placed the finger she'd pointed squarely in his chest.

"There may be a line of women from here to Hong Kong who have that intention. But I—" *poke* "—am—" *poke* "—not in it."

She stepped back, spent, her chest heaving. Even in his anger he had to admit that her argument had been eloquently delivered, and having run frustrated fingers through her hair, she'd never looked more beautiful. Her eyes were fiery, bringing to mind the things he did to make them look that way. But then he remembered that it was those moments of weakness that had led to him letting down his guard in the first place.

"Are you finished?"

Lauren telegraphed her answer by spinning around and walking away.

"Lauren, wait!"

She increased her speed. He watched as what had been a disappearing limp became more pronounced. He ran after her and clamped a hand on her shoulder.

"Baby, please, be careful! You'll reinjure your ankle."

She shook off his hand. "Oh, now you're concerned about me being in pain?"

"You act like I don't have a right to be angry!" He stopped himself. "Look, let's just both take some time to calm down, okay?"

"We can do more than that. During the remainder of my contract, we can both take steps to see each other as little as possible."

The comment stung, but Christian shook it off. He took a step toward her. "What about CANN Island?"

Lauren's chuckle held no humor. "Clearly, working together is out of the question."

Another step and then, "Don't be so hasty to throw away the chance of a lifetime. Even enemies can come together if they've a mind to."

"What, for the Breedlove business?" she hissed as she reached the driver's side of her car.

He pinned her against it. "No, for this."

The kiss was hot and hard, possessive and intense, so good it took both of their breaths away. She pushed him back and got into the car. He watched her drive away, his lips still sizzling from the intense oral exchange. Deep in thought, he hadn't realized that Victoria had walked up and joined him.

"A smart man never makes a decision without having all the facts," she said as the two continued to stare in the direction Lauren had driven.

"Are you saying that I should ignore the possibility of her planned duplicity after what I've gone through with others?"

Victoria placed a gentle hand on his arm. "No, son. I'm simply reminding you to be the smart man your father and I raised."

Nineteen

"She refused to allow me to abandon her. She actually used the word *abandon*!"

"You did say you wanted out of the contract, did you not?"

"Yes, but not without a way to ensure plans continued to run smoothly," Lauren huffed. "My leaving would have led to your promotion. Whose side are you on?"

Hours had passed since the meeting with Victoria, and Lauren was no less angry now than then—resentful at Victoria's insistence she stay here, outraged at Christian for kissing her and furious at her own body for its betrayal. Even now her skin longed for his touch. She'd called Frankie and asked him to come over. She wanted help moving but now, even more, could really use a friend.

"Girl, lower your pressure before you have a stroke."

Lauren threw up her hands in exasperation. "My blood pressure is fine, okay?"

"Ooh, girl, watch it!" Frankie hurried toward her.

Lauren waved away the concern. "Don't worry about my ankle. It's basically healed."

"I'm happy to hear that, but it's not your injury I'm worried about. It's that vase you keep walking by, flailing your arms all around. When I came by that first time, I thought it looked familiar so I looked it up online."

"And?"

"It's from the Song dynasty, darling, that's the bougie folk in China." At Frankie's insinuation that she was culturally clueless, Lauren rolled her eyes. "That piece right there is a gourd from the 12th or 13th century, so if you don't have six figures and a ticket to Shanghai, you might not want to break it."

"So it's not my health you're worried about, but a pretty piece of porcelain?"

"Absolutely." Said with not one ounce of shame.

With Frankie's help, packing went quickly. It was her clothes mostly, and what she'd bought to create a home office in the dining room. She was thankful for his constant chatter. It helped keep her mind off the fact that her and Christian's…whatever it was…was in tatters. She'd been angry that he hadn't believed her, but more, she'd been hurt at the thought of their friendship coming to an end. That was the real reason behind her jumbled feelings and the hole in her heart.

Later she'd think about temporary housing, but for now she went online and secured a hotel room in Henderson, Nevada. She rented a car, and Frankie drove her to get it. After helping her load her things in the trunk and promising he'd meet her at the foundation offices tomorrow, he left for a rendezvous with a guy he'd met online. There was only one thing left for Lauren to do.

She sat at the counter, opened her tablet and, after gathering her thoughts, began to type.

Victoria,
Please accept my apology for this afternoon's outburst. It's been a very challenging day. Despite the version you may have heard of what happened, I never meant to involve Christian in the drama. I have no ulterior motive for working with you. I am not out to trap your son. I respect him too much to ever do that and as much as I've tried to deny it, have developed true feelings for him, a fact that I hope can remain between us. That he thinks I've deceived him breaks my heart.

While I admit to wanting to immediately cut all ties with Breedlove, Nevada, I respect your insistence that I be a woman of my word. I enjoy working for the foundation, and with you, and will do my very best to make the remaining events not only successful, but the talk of the town.

Thank you so much for the generosity extended in offering one of your guesthouses for my stay. However, as of the writing of this note, I will no longer be here. I have made arrangements to live elsewhere, have secured a rental to get around and for the duration of the contract will work from the foundation offices. Considering the events that transpired today, and now knowing my true feelings for Christian, I'm sure you can understand. I remain eternally grateful for all you've done to help me and for the wonderful friendship you share with my mom. Until tomorrow...

Lauren hesitated only briefly before pressing Send. She closed the tablet, placed it in her tote, then took one last walk through her temporary home. It was the most beautiful residence in which she'd ever lived, and she was thankful to have stayed here. She'd miss it as much as or more than she'd miss the land itself. Most of all, she'd miss Christian, and would cherish the love affair that began within these walls. But life went on, and she had to move with it.

With a wistful sigh, she placed the card key on the counter, walked out of the front door, closed it softly behind her, and headed out of the Breedlove utopia and into the world where normal people lived.

The next day Lauren rose early, determined to get back to the business of the foundation and not deal with either her conflicting feelings for Christian or the drama involving her father on company time. It wouldn't be easy. Christian's kiss had seared her heart, branded her soul to the point that, except for dreams about him, she got no sleep at all. It wasn't just the sex she missed, she thoughtfully admitted. It was the man. A man whose absence left a void she doubted could be filled.

Fortunately for her, at least she'd be busy. It was roughly six weeks before the foundation's spring gala and there were a thousand details to handle between now and then. After showering, she blew dry and flat-ironed her hair, taking more care with her overall appearance. No longer working from home, and heading into halls undoubtedly roamed by upper-level millionaire executives, Lauren wanted to look the part, to fit right in. So after studying her options she'd decided on an ivory-colored wraparound dress, a strand of iridescent coral pearls she'd purchased in Djibouti, and even though she'd probably pay for it later, paired her braced sprained ankle with a three-inch ivory pump.

As with everything connected with the business of

Breedlove, the foundation offices were located at the CANN, smartly appointed facilities of varying sizes and configurations on the building's fifth floor. There were meeting rooms and establishments that catered to the hotel's corporate customers including an office supply store; a print, mail and shipping company; a luxury car rental; and a travel agency booking everything from first-class flights to private planes and helicopters.

Entering her office, Lauren was pleasantly surprised to see that Frankie had beaten her there. They hugged and she walked through the bright, airy, contemporary space and sat behind her desk. She probably should have come here sooner. Setting up in an office made her feel better and ready to work.

"You want something from the coffee shop?" Frankie asked. "I had a one-eye-open cup of java and I need another one to open the other eye."

"A caramel latte sounds delicious. And a bagel if they have it. Multigrain. Thanks."

Lauren moved a stack of files from her desk out to Frankie's. She stopped at the stereo panel, found some smooth jazz and returned to her desk. The silky saxophone notes that oozed into the room conjured up pictures of Christian, naked and sated, his eyes half-open, watching her. With a huff, Lauren pulled out her laptop. She'd just fired it up when she heard the door open. Not long enough for Frankie to have gotten the coffee already.

"All right, girlfriend. What did you forget?"

"To listen, maybe?"

Christian. Lauren slowly turned around as he strode toward her, looking like a cool drink of water on a hot summer day. She tamped down emotions and kept her face a mask.

"Maybe yesterday I judged you too harshly. I've been

burned a lot, and it's made me cynical. I hope you understand."

"Is that an apology?"

"Did you offer me one?"

They stared each other down, eyes blazing. Lauren blinked first, turned back to her computer. "I've got too much to do to deal with you right now. But just so you know, those listening skills still need work."

"Lauren, I'm sorry."

She could hear the effort that apology cost him, and turned back around. "Me, too. And while I've apologized before, I could also be more understanding. It was a terrible position to be in. You had every right to be angry."

"You're not the kind of woman who'd have to use any underhanded tactic to get a man, me or anyone else."

"Are those Victoria's words, or did you come to that conclusion on your own?"

"They're my words, but I'm sure Mom would agree with me. Dad, too, for that matter."

She watched him take a step toward her, saw his eyes darken and braced herself. "I missed you last night."

"Yeah," she whispered, barely audible. "Me, too."

"It's crazy. I dreamed of you."

"You did?" She swallowed the truth that tickled her throat, that she'd dreamed of him, too.

"Want to know what we were doing?"

Her smile matched his. "I think I can guess."

"We were back in Djibouti, in the glass-bottom boat. You were naked. And there, with some of the finest beauty in all of the world, all I saw was you."

Lauren's legs threatened to buckle beneath the sensuality of his dream. She abruptly sat and changed the subject. It was either that or close the door and take him on the desk.

"Thanks for stopping by, Christian. There's a ton of work to do in the next couple weeks, but I promise to get all the matter with Ed, and your part in it, straightened out."

"If you don't, I will."

"You won't have to," Lauren countered. "This is my business. I said I'd handle it, and I will."

"Okay."

They looked at each other. A second passed, then two. Their eyes conveyed words that didn't need to be spoken. Lauren inwardly admitted what she'd too long denied. She not only loved Christian Breedlove, she was falling in love with him.

He cleared his throat. "Speaking of business, listen. You've got skills that the company can use, and from the sound of things your being in Vegas is beneficial to you, too. So let's try to focus on work when we're working and handle personal affairs when we're not on the clock. Fair enough?"

"That's fair."

Just then, Lauren noticed a leather-bound portfolio Christian carried. He held it out to her.

She reached for it. "What's this?"

"A proposed contract for you to work on CANN Island. Look it over, run it past your attorney, make any changes you desire. After that we can meet and hammer out the official version for your signature."

Lauren flipped through the pages. "When do you need this back?"

"The sooner, the better. While part of CANN International, we want the island project to have its own special branding with a cool tagline, such as what you designed for the jewelry video. We want to get brochures done and videos shot. Collateral for both investors and visitors, too."

"Sounds like a lot of work, especially on top of what I'm already doing for Victoria and the foundation."

"I understand, and when working on major events, the foundation will still be your priority," he reassured her. "What I'm asking for should come during the foundation's downtimes, depending on how much time you'll need for the projects I'm proposing. It'll take a bit of adjusting on both our parts, but I believe we can work it out."

"I do, too."

Christian nodded and headed for the door.

"Christian."

"Yes?"

"Thank you."

His eyes darkened as they slid from her eyes to her lips. Quivers traveled from her core to her nether set. For several seconds neither spoke, but again, messages were communicated.

"You're welcome."

He left. Lauren let out the breath she didn't know she'd been holding. How could she work beside that man and not be intimate when her entire body craved his touch? It was a question she mulled over all day long but even after midnight, as she crawled into bed, she didn't have the answer.

Twenty

"**B**ig brother!" Said in stereo by Noah and Nick as they burst through the private entrance to his spacious office without bothering to knock.

"The dynamic duo," Christian said drily. "Ill-mannered and uninvited. Just what I need."

"You'll take back those words in a minute." Noah plopped into one of two chairs facing Christian's desk, with complete irreverence for the superlight gray cashmere Enzo D'Orsi original that had set him back almost six figures. "We've got an idea that will blow your mind!"

"And some great news to go along with it!" Nick added. He reached into a crystal bowl of mints, unraveled the plastic wrapper and popped it in his mouth.

Great news? He could use some. Lauren's betrayal had left him in a serious funk. Even now, days after he and Lauren came to a tenuous truce and with him finally believing the story about why she lied, the deception had put an unsightly mark on a woman he thought could be the missus. If he were looking for such a thing. Which he wasn't.

You're married to CANN, remember?

With all of the other women, this line had worked. He'd said it, and he'd meant it. But not today. His heart literally ached at the thought that the possibility of a lifetime with Lauren had been destroyed. But this was a personal matter, and he was on the clock. So he took a deep breath, forced his mind back on business and hid his angst beneath a casual smile.

"I have a feeling I could live to regret this but, all right, what's this bright idea?"

"CANN Isles," Noah began dramatically.

"Oh, like the one being planned in Djibouti? Were it not for the fact that Noah sat in on the quite extensive sales presentation, I'd say great minds think alike. Instead I'll just say…get out."

"Not so fast, thundercloud," Nick said. "We know you're proud of that latest baby, especially since our phones are blowing up with interested investors from all over the world."

Noah sat up and leaned forward, fixing Christian with a laser stare. "So, check this out. CANN Island is the deluxe version, in Djibouti, right? And on private islands dotted across the country, smaller versions of your grand idea will become known as… CANN Isles. Off of the most scenic coasts of every continent. Genius, right?"

Christian looked between the twins, searched for the twinkle in their eye that would tell him they were joking. They were not.

"You do know that isn't a novel idea, that people buy islands and build mansions on them."

"Right, mansions. Not hotels. And not like us."

"There may be a reason," Christian countered. "Like not wanting to sink a building of high-paying guests into the big blue."

He looked at his watch, fired up his computer and began going over notes for a meeting taking place in an hour.

"You're not getting it," Nick said. He hopped out of the chair and paced the room. "We're talking boutique hotels—limited number of rooms, very exclusive."

"With perks and amenities unparalleled," Noah said, counting on his fingers. "Butlers, private chefs, complimentary top-shelf drinks and a bottle of premium Dom on arrival."

"Isle to land service via a customized private plane."

Christian harrumphed with a slight headshake. *Offering my plane as part of guest perks? Kids... I swear.*

"I was in New York over the weekend," Nick said, following his brother in typical tag team fashion. "And a unique opportunity presented itself. A private island, ten square miles, with a view of Manhattan."

"What was the opportunity?" Christian asked.

"It was for sale, just came on the market," Nick replied. "And I bought it."

This got Christian's attention. He leaned back in his chair, watched as the twins shared a cocky smile between them and felt a little burst of pride in his chest. "Okay, duo dudes, tell me more."

For the next thirty minutes the twins shared their vision. When they finished, Christian was more than intrigued. "Put something together for Dad and me," he told them. "Do either of you have something pressing in the next hour or so?"

They both shook their heads.

"Good, I think it would be beneficial to have you two in this meeting."

He reached for the office phone, a sign of dismissal. The twins took the hint and quietly exited the room. Christian wanted them gone but there really was a call to make, to one more person who should be in the meeting. Lauren.

She arrived just moments before the start of his presentation and took his breath away. Her look was simple sophistication, impeccable. He never dreamed a tailored business suit could look so sexy. Her hair was still straightened, but today it was pulled into a high ponytail that emphasized her almond-shaped eyes and high cheekbones. Red lipstick boldly brought attention to her succulent lips. He watched the men pause as she walked into the room and VP Greg Chapman become a bumbling idiot as he rushed to pull back her chair. Noah sidled over with admiring eyes taking her in, leaned down and said something that made Lauren laugh.

Christian wanted to kiss her and choke him.

"All right, gang," Christian began a few minutes later. "Let's get started. Some of you have met Lauren Hart." He gestured toward her. She nodded, a pleasant, professional look on her face as she made eye contact with the eight people at the table besides Christian and her.

"Lauren relocated from the East Coast to help Victoria Breedlove with a series of CANN Foundation fund-raisers, an important component of the overall organization and one that helps thousands of people live better lives, both here in the state of Nevada and around the world.

"Two weeks ago the foundation held its annual fashion show and tea, and thanks to Lauren's uniquely creative marketing expertise, it became the most profitable fund-raiser in the ten years the foundation has been in operation."

He waited a beat to let that fact sink in, and watched respect and admiration be added to the subtle look of lust in their eyes.

"I had a chance to view part of Ms. Hart's campaign and got an idea of why the event experienced record-breaking success and immediately thought that skill set could be advantageous to CANN International as we move forward with several new ventures, the first of which is CANN Island.

"As some of you know, Ms. Hart and I recently traveled to Djibouti for a series of meetings, all of which went quite well. The government is well aware of what a business like ours can do for their economy, and they've been extremely welcoming and helpful. I also met with several investors and potential partners for the retail and entertainment aspects of the overall plan, all of which I've condensed into a report that by the time you return to your offices will be in your inbox." He cleared his throat. "However, for right now I'd like to formally welcome Lauren to the team and ask her to say a word or two regarding her thoughts on the visit and our future in African tourism." He watched her eyes flare briefly at the unexpected request, even as she scooted her chair away from the table. "Lauren?"

Lauren stood and joined Christian at the front of the room. "Do we have any Boy Scouts?" she asked, holding up her hand.

A couple men held up a hand or a finger.

"I was a Girl Scout, and those of you who were Boy Scouts know the motto that was drilled into our learning experience. Be Prepared. That advice has served me well throughout the years, as it does now in being called upon for an impromptu presentation." She looked at Christian with a deceptively kind smile. "I'm prepared."

The men laughed and even the couple she saw who for whatever reason were clearly not happy seemed to loosen up a bit. She was confident and well-spoken as she gave a brief bio that included personal information such as her western roots, her college education and awards, and her professional history that included work with Fortune 100 and 500 companies.

"I believe there are some things that can't be taught," she finished, "or even learned. And while I appreciate both my higher learning and the experience I've gained, my uniquely creative way with words, as Christian put it, I believe is a gift, something that's always come naturally. I was thrilled to learn that the ideas put forth for the Valentine's Day fashion and tea resulted in a record-breaking fund-raiser. I look forward to working on the for-profit side of CANN and breaking even more."

Christian scanned the room as Lauren spoke, his coworkers, peers, in the palm of her hand. He was no exception. It was the first time he'd witnessed her in a corporate environment. He'd been enthralled, smitten, while watching her effortlessly navigate the high-ticket fashion show's rarefied air. But here, on his boardroom turf, she was just as natural and even more impressive. Beautiful and smart, a winning combination. Even for a woman he couldn't marry. He ignored the errant thought, focused on her lips and remembered the long moments he'd gotten lost just kissing them. When he knocked on her office door an hour later, kissing was still very much on his mind.

"Hey, beautiful," he said when she beckoned him in. Lauren made a face. "Sorry, I forgot. It's business hours. Hey, Lauren."

He was rewarded with a smirky smile. "Mr. Breedlove, how can I help you?"

"By joining me for lunch."

"I wasn't planning on taking a lunch. Being at the meeting and learning more about CANN was very beneficial, but it took a chunk out of my workday."

Lauren came out from behind her desk to place a book on the history of casinos and the Las Vegas Strip back on the office's well-organized shelves. "I think I'll go online, check out the restaurant menus and have something delivered."

When she turned, Christian was there, a hair's breadth away. "It's not good to work on an empty stomach," he whispered. "I think we should...eat."

He leaned over and removed the inch of distance between their mouths, capturing the lips that back in the boardroom had driven him insane. Lauren responded as he'd hoped she would, stepping closer, her hands running up his chest to encircle his neck. He brought his hand up to the delicious peaks that he loved to swirl with his tongue, slid his hand beneath her top and under her bra. Lauren moaned. His manhood swelled. She began grinding against it, undid his belt and reached for his zipper. The movement made him as hard as a rock. Then she stopped.

"No," she mumbled, stepping away from him. "We can't do that. I can't. Not here, not now. There's still so much uncertainty, so much to work out."

"I'm sorry."

"Don't be. I wanted it. I still do."

"Lunch, then..." Lauren shook her head. "No private room. I'll even do fast food in the main casino, surrounded by hundreds of tourists and clanging slot machines."

"Somehow that's impossible to envision. You being handed a hot dog and fries in a paper bag."

"If it meant spending more time with you," he drawled, "I'd eat the paper bag."

Lauren returned to her chair behind the desk. "You're not making this easy."

"I hope not."

She walked around the desk and reached for her purse. "Where are we going?"

His smile was as bright as sunshine. "That's my girl."

They bypassed the upscale food court and settled on a restaurant boasting American fusion cuisine and run by a celebrity chef. They ordered their meals and in a mutual yet unspoken agreement climbed above the touchier matters to safe, innocuous subjects.

Lauren stopped eating a scrumptious salmon salad and wiped her mouth. "Did you ever want to do anything else?" At his genuinely confused look, she added, "You know, besides working for the family business?"

Christian smiled and shook his head. "No, never. From my earliest memories, I worshipped Dad, wanted to be just like him, do everything he did. I vividly remember getting my first suit—three piece, navy—an exact replica of one that he wore. I cried when it was time for bed and Mom said to take it off. She had to threaten me with a spanking before I obeyed her."

"Oh my gosh! How old were you?"

Christian rubbed his chin. "Three, almost four."

"I can only imagine. You were a handful."

He fixed her with a look. "I still am."

The atmosphere shifted. Both tried to ignore it. But when they simultaneously reached for the salt and their fingers touched, the truth couldn't be denied. The attraction was still there—strong, powerful and hotter than ever.

Twenty-One

Strained didn't begin to describe the next few weeks. Lauren saw Christian more than ever. They worked out a deal for her participation in the Djibouti CANN Island project. Not much work, really. Christian made her an offer she'd be a fool to refuse. She'd earn twice the money that she'd made anywhere else while putting in fewer hours for CANN International and enjoying the perks of a full-time employee.

Only once had he asked about her father and Ed, and if she'd told them about the fake marriage. He was constantly traveling and immersed in plans for CANN Island. Work seemed to have pushed what happened to the back of his mind. For Lauren, however, the situation remained at the forefront and continued to loom large over her happiness. Ed continued to harass her, threatening to out her father's dark deed and calling her marriage to Christian a sham. "Why can't I find anything online?"

he'd asked. This weekend he'd have his answer. Lauren would tell the truth and let the chips fall where they may.

As the plane neared the airport and began to descend, she looked out the window. The gray skies and raindrops sliding down the small windows seemed appropriate as they mirrored her feelings exactly. Conflicting emotions warred inside her, and it was hard to know what to feel. In the moment, she was numb, feeling nothing at all as thoughts chased memories, bumped against each other and then melted together, becoming one endless scenario of despair and ecstasy, frustration and chaos.

The pressure in her ears increased as the plane continued lower. She worked her jaws to pop them, watched as the silvery ribbons turned into highways and the green swaths became lawns and trees. Was it really less than two months ago that she flew to where Christian's jet had been customized, and then touched down in Vegas on his birthday to escape her old life and search for a new one? Where her preteen crush turned into the greatest whirlwind romance of her life only to dissipate in an equally short time? And the biggest question of all: Could they rise above the drama, have their lust turn into love, and have their flickering desire become a lasting flame?

Unlike Thanksgiving or Christmas, Easter travel was the same as any regular weekend in the nation's capital. Lauren had only brought a carry-on for the long weekend she'd be at home and made it through Washington National rather quickly. On the way from the Jetway she'd texted her mom, who pulled up curbside within minutes of her nearing the exit. She withstood the steady drizzle sans umbrella, threw her carry-on into the back seat and gave her mom a hug.

Faye hugged her back tightly. "It's so good to see you, honey."

"It's good to see you, too. Although honestly, I was less than excited to come back home."

"Given the circumstances, I'd feel the same way." Faye checked her rearview mirror and eased away from the curb. "I'm so sorry about everything that's happened. So is your father. After what happened in Las Vegas, he took a good look at Ed, asked around about him. The co-workers didn't hold back."

"What did they say?" Lauren asked.

"That he's a jerk, basically, the same as you said. Paul went to Ed and told him that he no longer supported his desire to marry you. Despite what may happen to him, Paul demanded he leave you alone."

"That couldn't have been easy."

"No, and it didn't go over well."

"What happened?"

"Ed reiterated his threat to tell Gerald about the embezzlement. That's when your father turned the tables."

"How?"

"Just yesterday, he called a meeting with Ed and Gerald and told him everything."

Lauren whispered, "Oh my God."

"From what transpired after that, the man upstairs was definitely present. Gerald isn't going to press charges, honey."

Lauren dropped her head in her hands. "Thank God!"

"He was hurt, very hurt, and disappointed. But Paul told him the whole story without holding back—about the fledgling business, even after Gerald's investment, the mortgages on the house and Ed's threats. Gerald was really angry about that. He couldn't believe his son would try to blackmail someone into marrying him. I think that's what really gave Gerald the compassion to forgive Paul and accept restitution instead of pressing charges."

Lauren sat silent, too stunned to react. This news changed everything! With Ed's threat no longer a cloud over her head, she could reveal the sham to him and then go on with her life. She could think about a future in Breedlove, Nevada. She could think of a lifetime with Christian.

"Did Dad lose his job?" she finally asked.

Faye shook her head. "Paul offered his resignation but Gerald refused it, again showing what kind of true friend he is. It's hard to believe an apple like Ed fell from that tree. He did order a full audit, though. And there will be financial oversight from an outside company for the next five years. Paul will have to pay for that. But all in all, given what could have happened, this is an outcome beyond what we could have dreamed."

As the conversation shifted to other topics, Lauren's mood lifted. She took in the city with brighter eyes. She noticed the last of the cherry blossoms on thin, bobbing branches and appreciated the blending of old and new in the city's regentrifying neighborhoods. They reached the wide avenues of Brandywine, with its large manicured lawns and white oak and Virginia pine trees. The Harts' home on the corner lot anchored their block. Tall, white and imposing with black shutters and gleaming glass, multicolored flowers against the wrought iron fence, and a red cobblestoned drive made it stand out, a fitting tribute to what the upper-class builders had in mind when development of the tony area began. Lauren's heart swelled with gratitude. The threat was over. Her parents would not lose their home.

After placing her luggage into her old bedroom, now a guest room, Lauren called Ed. She put the call on speaker, pacing as she waited for him to answer the phone.

"Hello?"

"Ed, it's Lauren."

"Lauren. To what do I owe the pleasure?"

Lauren ignored the attitude in his voice and responded as pleasantly as she could. "I just talked with Mom. She told me what happened, that Dad told your father the truth. I wanted to share a truth as well."

"What, that you'll marry me?"

Lauren plopped on the bed she'd slept in for years. "Ed, you don't want to marry me. You just don't like to lose. There is someone out there for you. Someone who can do more for you and your image than I ever could. I know you love moving and shaking in the tristate area, and I've extended my contract in Nevada. I'll be staying out west. You need someone here, a socialite, someone who'll look good on your arm and wants to be there."

She waited, hoped for a civil exchange. No matter how she felt about Ed, his father, Gerald, was a man she greatly respected. Not many in his position would have forgiven her father and kept him employed.

"What if I'm not ready to let you go?"

"You can't hold on to what you've never had. There is no chance of a romance between us. We need to end this madness, now."

"Or what?" Lauren could hear Ed's rising anger through the phone. "You going to sic the Breedlove brothers on me? Well, let me tell you something, baby. I'm not afraid of those effeminate dudes. And if they ever come east, on my turf, they'll find that out."

She ignored the jab, refused to take the bait. "Speaking of the Breedloves, I have a confession to make."

"You're not married to that asshole," he hissed. "I already know."

"I lied because I felt pressured, like my back was against the wall."

"Lies can get you into trouble."

"I know, which is why I wanted to clear everything up."

"Consider it cleared."

"So this is it? The harassment's over?"

"You have nothing I want," he said.

"I wish you the best, Ed."

"Have fun out west."

The cordiality in his voice was obviously fake, a tone that gave her the chills. She tried to dismiss the foreboding feeling. But as she ended the call, she couldn't deny the truth: *that was much too easy.*

A veritable feast was being prepared at the Breedlove estate. The family gathered for a down-home cooked meal on the northwest side of the property at Papa Will Yazzie and Grandma Breedlove Yazzie's rambling single-story farmhouse. It was one of a few times of year that Grandma Jewel forbade "chef anybody" or "catered anything" to darken her door. Christian knew that Easter was one of his grandmother's favorite holidays. It reminded her of childhood—frilly dresses, colored Easter eggs and speeches at a small Methodist church.

For Papa Will, Grandma's second husband who had Native American roots, the holiday held less meaning. But he'd do anything to make "my Jewel" happy. And so would she for him, which is why the following weekend they'd head to New Mexico for the Gathering of Nations annual powwow.

Today, extended family from both sides had traveled from as close as California and as far away as Texas. Inside, the women ruled and in the kitchen, Grandma Jewel's domain, she was the captain of a mountain of sides—dressing, salads, macaroni and cheese—and it was all hands on deck. Even Victoria, who rarely stepped into any of the three kitchens located in her home, sat at the table, chatting with her mom Sylvia, dutifully and daintily separating the yolks from the whites of hard-boiled eggs for her sister's famous deviled eggs.

Outside, the brothers enjoyed hanging out with their cousins and friends. Nick and Noah played touch football with a group of their peers while Adam and some of the others attempted polo a short distance away. Others sipped beer and other libations on the wraparound porch. That's where Christian sat, keeping company with Papa Will, watching as he carefully basted a slow-roasting pig on a spit and listening as he spilled secrets on how he and Jewel kept the home fires burning and the love alive. "Humor and humility, mostly," he crooned, while basting the beast.

Cuts of beef and whole chickens sat on the grill; a whole turkey set dressed for the fryer, the smell of hickory and burning wood filling the air. His gaze drifted from Papa Will to the mountain in the distance, the one where after visiting their childhood cave Lauren had been thrown from the horse. He allowed the truth of the matter to fill his mind. He missed her, desperately. Reaching for his phone, he walked a distance into the yard as he hit the speaker button.

"Hey, beautiful."

"Christian, hi!"

"Wow, you sound happy. The East must be agreeing with you."

"I've never felt better." She gave Christian an update of what had happened over the past few days. "I can't believe that it's over. I'm so relieved."

"So am I."

"I know I've said it more than once but again, I'm really sorry for lying and putting you in such an awkward position."

"You did what you had to do. That's behind us now. Let's have it stay there. When are you coming home?"

"My flight leaves at seven and arrives at McCarran just after eleven," she answered.

"Text me the itinerary. I'll pick you up."

"You don't have to."

"I want to. And just so you know, you're coming home with me and spending the night. No argument. No excuses."

"I wouldn't offer any because there's no other place I'd rather be. I'll see you later, then?"

"You can count on it, beautiful."

Christian hung up the phone and joined the rest of the family gathering on the porch as dinner was served. There was more food, drink and laughter than he'd seen in a while. He was happy, almost giddy. There was one reason. Lauren.

At a little past nine, he hugged everyone goodbye and headed home to shower and change to meet Lauren at the airport. He was pleased to see her smiling face within moments of reaching the passenger pickup lane. Before he could exit the car she'd opened the back door and thrown her carry-on inside.

"I was going to do that for you," he drawled, soaking her up with his eyes.

She leaned over. "I know. I'm in a hurry. It's time to get wet."

The verbal nod to their earlier encounters was all the encouragement Christian needed to test his car's horsepower. He didn't have to check the speedometer to know that night he broke the law. Conversation was minimal during the short drive to Breedlove. They exited the car, giggling like teenagers as they pulled at clothes and each other from the garage to the great room. That first coming together was urgent, almost frantic, Lauren splayed across the back of the leather couch, urging him to take her from behind.

He pressed his tip against the wet entry beckoning him forward, then stopped.

"No!"

"Wait, baby. I need a condom."

"I can't wait," Lauren panted as she turned and reached for the massive hard shaft that was hot to the touch.

Her pleading was something he couldn't deny. He placed his hands on her hips, spun her back around and sank into paradise. The unfettered rawness of skin against skin drove the relentless pounding, along with Lauren's moans and growled commands. He squeezed her cheeks and slowed the rhythm to match the swivel of her hips. It was a perfectly executed dance for which they hadn't rehearsed, yet performed as though having done it a thousand times. When he reached for Lauren's silky folds, slid a finger between them and massaged her pearl, she came undone. He wasn't far behind. The reunion was super climactic, but they were just getting started.

"Come here," Lauren whispered when she'd regained her breath.

"Where are we going?"

She didn't answer, just reached for his hand and headed to the master suite. Once there she continued to the customized shower, stared at the various knobs and showerheads.

"How do you work this thing?"

Christian laughed. "What do you want? A single flow, duel pumps, a rain forest effect?"

"Definitely the rain forest."

Christian turned on the water and joined Lauren beneath the flow. She poured bath soap into her hand and then, forgoing a sponge, used her body as the friction to unleash the bubbly scent. That done, her eyes locked with his, she began a trail of kisses. His neck, pecs, abs, hips, until taking his hardened heat in her hands and stroking its length as she stuck out her tongue and outlined his perfectly mushroomed tip. Over, and again, before taking him in, her warm cavern causing goose bumps all over his skin. She lavished him from head to toe. Then he returned the favor. As trails of orange, purple, pink and blue announced the dawn, Christian and Lauren climbed into his bed, wrapped themselves around each other and fell into what was for both the first night of dreamless sleep in a while.

Twenty-Two

Lauren awoke with a smile on her face. She looked over at Christian, who was also awake, also smiling and looking at her.

"Hey."

"Hello, beautiful."

She rolled into his arms. "Did last night really happen?"

"All the way into the morning."

"Ha!" Lauren sat up and stretched. "I feel amazing! Oh, but wait a minute."

"What?"

"What about our stateside rule?"

"What about the friends-with-benefits exception?"

"Right. It's kind of like having our cake and eating it, too."

Christian shifted his body and kissed her breasts. "Speaking of…are you hungry? Because I could definitely eat again."

"Something tells me you're not talking about a dish that the chef can cook up."

"Naw, you rule this particular kitchen."

Lauren slid down alongside Christian. Just as they began to kiss, his cell phone rang. He looked over, saw that it was Adam and declined the call with one of the prepared messages. Busy. Call you later. Within seconds, his text and email notifications began going off like crazy. He frowned, reached for the phone and placed his finger on the fingerprint scanner to unlock it. Figuring that the texts and emails could be part of a scam, he instead tapped the screen to return Adam's missed call. He put the call on speaker and pulled Lauren into his arms.

"What's up, bro?" he asked.

"There's no easy way to tell you," Adam replied. "But you need to brace yourself. Because your fake wedding is all over the news."

"What?" Adam's words sat Lauren straight up.

"Is that Lauren?" Adam asked.

"Hey, Adam. Yeah, it's me. What's going on?"

"That's what you need to tell my brother. Christian, I sent one of the links to your phone. You need to check it out… ASAP."

The line went dead. Christian turned and looked at her. His expression was confused, yet cold. She could tell he fought to stay calm.

"Well?"

"Christian, I swear I don't know what's going on."

He got out of bed, donned a pair of shorts and reached for his phone. He scrolled the face, reading whatever Adam sent him, she presumed. His jaw clenched in anger. She got out of bed.

"What does it say?"

"You didn't talk to anyone back east?"

"Only the conversation with Ed that I told you about. Where I admitted to having lied about being married."

"Where did the conversation take place?"

"Over the phone. What are they saying in the article?"

"Not what you said you told Ed. Put on your clothes. This party is over. I'll take you back to your place where you can read it for yourself."

Lauren went in search of her clothes. By the time she'd slipped into them Christian was dressed, too, with keys in hand.

"Christian, wait." She whipped out her phone, did a quick internet search on Christian's name and clicked on the first link that appeared.

"You can't possibly believe I had anything to do with this," she said, after reading the first damaging paragraph.

"You told me the conversation with Ed was cordial, that he agreed to leave you alone."

"He did, but…" Lauren's words trailed off as she remembered the feeling that came over her when their call ended. "He said everything was fine and I desperately wanted to believe it, so I convinced myself that saga was over and done. But I felt something was wrong, off, about his demeanor. Like the resolution was almost too easy. This had to have been Ed's doing, Christian. He probably had it planned all along, as revenge if I told him no."

She looked at Christian, her eyes filled with regret. "Baby, I'm so sorry."

"I am, too. Let's go."

"I don't want to leave you, Christian. Not like this. Why don't I stay so that we can work through this together?"

"Maybe later," he said. "Right now there's work to

do—conferencing and strategizing with attorneys and publicists. We've got a few fires to put out."

The drive from his house to the hotel was done in total silence. He pulled into the circular entrance and waved away the valet coming to greet them. Christian put the car in Park and after a long moment, held out his arms. Lauren fell into them and fought back tears.

"I'm sorry, baby," he said, moving his hands from around her and placing her away from him "I know this leak isn't your fault, but I can't help thinking that the lie you told Ed was the basis for this story." He held up a hand to stop her protest. "I'm not saying that what I'm thinking is right or even rational. What's happened in the past affects my present. And because of that, I can't be with you right now."

"So this time it's you putting the brakes on our making love?"

"I guess so." He put the car in Drive, a sign that their conversation was over. "But tomorrow it will be business as usual. I'll see you at work."

Lauren maintained her composure until she entered her room, then allowed the tears to flow. She pulled out her phone to call Avery and was surprised to see missed texts and calls. Only then did she realize she'd been so excited to see Christian that she'd never taken her phone out of airplane mode. When she did, she wished she hadn't. The sham marriage wasn't the blogger's only news. Her father's indiscretion had also been exposed.

Lauren called home. Faye answered the phone, distraught as Lauren imagined she'd be.

"Your father is holed up in the study," Faye finished. "I'm worried about him, Lauren. He's totally broken."

"Mom, I'm so sorry," Lauren cried, tears falling again. "It's all my fault."

"Ed Miller is to blame for this. I'd bet everything I own that he was behind this article. Your dad stood up to him, and he couldn't stand it."

"Should I come back home? Do you think Dad would feel better if I talked to him?"

"Nothing can help right now, dear. Except prayer. Will you do that?"

It had been a while since their last conversation, but when Lauren ended the call with Faye she closed her eyes and asked God for the biggest favor in her entire life.

The next day Lauren and Victoria met in the Breedloves' home. Victoria was gracious, as usual. She could afford to be more objective than her son. The family had endured greater scandals, she assured Lauren, and said no doubt there'd be more. She even offered the guesthouse back for Lauren's extended stay. But Lauren moved out of the hotel in Henderson and found a condo to sublet not far from the Strip and threw herself into work for the foundation.

When at the hotel working with Christian, she hid her heartache at his distance behind a professional veneer. Did she miss making love with him? Absolutely. Did she think it was possible for them to have a relationship? No idea. Lauren couldn't figure out her own feelings, much less try to meld them with someone else's. She was worried about her parents, who'd indeed retained legal counsel, even though Gerald penned a response that blasted his own son. Fortunately for her, the foundation's second major gala—a Saturday-night concert during Memorial Day weekend—was taking place in just three weeks. Between overseeing that project and working on CANN Island, she had precious little time to think of Christian, how much she missed him or if she would ever feel his arms around her again.

The following Monday, her second week back in Nevada and first full day in the office at CANN, Lauren worked twelve hours. She was exhausted but felt immense satisfaction from being in control of something she was good at and getting things done. Being the last person in the office, she turned off the lights, locked up and headed to executive parking, dreaming of Chinese takeout, a long, hot shower and a good night's sleep.

"Hello, Lauren."

Lauren turned toward the voice, where the private elevator doors had just opened. Even without turning around she would have known it was Christian. He looked good enough to eat and as tired as she was, she still wanted to.

"Hey."

"Trying to avoid me?" he asked.

"No."

Lauren continued toward her car.

Christian fell in alongside her. "Just another day at the office, burning the midnight oil?"

"I got the email about the meeting next week and was getting a head start on my presentation. With the upcoming concert, this was one of the only days I could focus on CANN Island."

"Your work is impressive. Even my haters have taken notice."

"Phillip Troutman and Wally Long?" she guessed.

"Ha! You figured them out already?"

"I pay attention." They reached her car. "I also saw the retraction by the blogger who released that initial article about my dad and our supposed marriage, and the article your publicist wrote stating the facts. Your kind words were a boost to my father's spirits, and while you could have raked me over the coals, you didn't. That was very kind of you, and I appreciate it."

"I hate that Ed told the blogger I actually got married and other papers reported the lie. Scandal can affect business. But as Mom has so eloquently pointed out several times recently, it comes with the territory of being a Breedlove. Back then you did what you felt you had to do, and what subsequently got leaked was not your fault."

"Thank you."

Lauren reached for the door handle. Christian blocked her.

"Where are you headed?"

"Home, thank God."

"Where's that," Christian asked, "since you turned down Mom's offer to return to the guesthouse?"

"Not far," was Lauren's evasive answer.

"Listen to you, trying to sound all mysterious."

"That was a polite way to suggest that you mind your business."

"Ha!"

Lauren smiled. "I'm kidding."

"No, you're not. But that straightforwardness is pretty sexy."

"Hmm."

"Come with me."

"Where are we going?"

Christian gently took her arm and led her a couple cars down, to a pearl-white sedan.

"To get something to eat."

Christian pulled out a key fob. Lauren heard a *click*. He held the door open.

"This is you?" He shut her door, then went around to the driver's side and got in. "You got another car?"

"I'm thinking about it. Trying it out."

Lauren looked at the steering wheel and saw a symbol she'd seen before. Not in person, but in magazines, and on television a time or two.

"This is a Bentley?" He nodded. "No wonder the leather feels so amazing. But look how it's streaked. They must have used the cheap stuff."

Her jab did as intended and caused Christian to flash his flawless smile. The beauty of those pearly whites against his dark skin, framed by those nice lips, was like a cup of caffeine straight into her core. That fine brother gave her life!

"It's a way of treating the leather that retains the hide's natural essence."

"It's beautiful, but so not politically correct."

"Definitely not for everyone."

So focused on the car's interior, she didn't pay attention to where they were going until Christian pressed on the gas, and the power generated by the twin-turbo engines forced her back against the seat. They'd merged onto Interstate 15, headed toward Breedlove.

"Are we going to the estate?" Christian shook his head. "Where then?"

"We're going to hang out with the Breedlove locals."

She arched a brow. "Isn't that what I've been doing for the past two months?"

"You've been in the inner circle of the town's elite. We're going to hang out with regular folk."

Lauren relaxed against the headrest, watched Christian's strong, capable fingers work the stereo system until the soft sounds of neo soul filled the air. She remembered the last time those hands had touched her body, the night she'd returned from Maryland and they'd made love all night long. Aside from music delivered so crisply it sounded as though the artist was in the back seat, there was no other noise. No sound of tires rolling on cement, no hum of engine, no sound of wind. Before, she'd felt it a complete waste of money to spend as much on a car as some did on their houses. But now as the beast quietly ate up the highway, she understood why some did. Riding in the Bentley was like floating on a cloud. That Christian was beside her made it feel a bit like heaven. But Lauren knew that, sadly, there was no reclaiming that paradise. Even though he knew that Ed leaked the story, Lauren owned her part in the matter, that had she never lied in the first place there wouldn't have been a story. Could Christian ever truly forgive her for that? And did she want to be with a man who couldn't forgive, forget and move on?

They drove past the estate and into the town of Breedlove, population 2,137. The main street, called Main Street, was straight out of a movie, Mayberry in the twenty-first century. A bank anchored one corner, with a small grocer on the other. Lauren glimpsed a doughnut shop, an insurance company, a consignment store and a dollar mart before Christian turned the corner onto Sixth Street, the second main drag. Several cars lined this street. Young people mingled between them. Two guys tossed a neon football. Loud music played. She tried to imagine Christian as one of these kids. She couldn't.

"So this is where you grew up, huh?" Lauren murmured.

"Yes and no. I went to a private high school in Las Vegas, so my interaction with kids my age here in Breedlove was limited. Plus there was the whole 'rich kid' stereotype, and people thinking I thought more of myself than I did." He exhaled. "Add to that the other guys' girlfriends always coming at me and you end up with someone the other guys would rather not have around."

"Sounds rather lonely."

"Hardly. Who needed them? I had my brothers. Those who were welcomed into our gang were the lucky ones."

Lauren would have called him cocky or conceited, except she knew what he'd said was true.

They pulled up to a '50s-style burger joint with two huge *B*s outlined in neon lights.

"What's that stand for?" Lauren asked, after Christian had come around and opened her door.

"Breedlove Burgers."

"Another family business," she teased. He nodded. "Really? I was just joking."

They entered the noisy establishment, which smelled of caramelized onions and grilled beef. Private school aside, Christian seemed to know everyone in the place. He spoke to them all on the way to a booth at the back of the room. A server came for their order, which he placed without asking what Lauren wanted. "Trust me," he said, to her raised-eyebrow question.

She did. "You guys really own this place?"

"Not us. My brother Adam. This is his baby."

"I never would have taken him for a restaurateur."

"It's a way for him to show off the beef he raises."

Lauren shook her head. "You lost me."

"Adam's a cowboy, and a rancher. You've been to his place and didn't figure that out?"

"I saw dozens of cattle that day out running but it didn't occur to me that they belonged to Adam. Is there anything your family can't do?"

"No."

Over double burgers on toasted buns and home-cut fries, Lauren learned about the history of Breedlove and the part Christian's dad, Nicholas, played in founding the town. It was quite a backstory, which left her even

more impressed with the family than she already was…
which was a lot.

"Do you think we could work together?" Lauren
hadn't meant to ask the question aloud and even as she
had, knew he'd misinterpret its meaning.

"We do work together, Lauren."

"Not professionally, but personally. Do you think you
and I could have a successful relationship, or do you
think our personalities are too explosive for it to ever
work out?"

"Wow, what brought that on?"

"The decision to be honest with myself, and to be as
honest with you as I was with Ed when I told him I didn't
want to be with him." She rested a hand on his arm. "I
do want to be with you, and if you feel the same, I would
love to see where having a real relationship might take
us. Is that possible?"

"I don't know."

His smoldering look seared her insides even as his
answer squeezed her heart.

"I'll admit that what we have is special. You're an
amazing woman who's caused me to consider things I've
never thought about before. Having just been promoted
to the helm of CANN, I had no plans to get into a relationship. Yet even though we've never said it, that feels
like what this is."

"I feel the same way, too," she whispered.

"But the truth is, everything that's happened recently
makes the matter more complicated. I'm already high
profile and don't know that I'm ready for the spotlight
that would come with dating the woman named in the
blog that went viral, exposing deception. I've forgiven
you," he quickly added. "What I'm saying isn't personal,
but viewed strictly from my position as president of a

company where profile matters. It may sound cold to
hear me put business before love, but I have more than
myself to think about. I have my family, hundreds of
employees, their families, investors…" A look of ach-
ing regret crossed his handsome face. "What happens
to me reflects on the company, for better or worse. Any
scandal in my personal life is seen by my professional
peers. Maybe later, after the CANN Island launch, when
the rumor mill has tired of the sham marriage story, I'll
feel more comfortable taking the chance. But right now
is not that time. Can you understand that?"

Lauren nodded, squared her shoulders and placed a
shield over her heart. "I can totally understand it."

He held out his hand. "Friends?"

She slid her hand into his and braced herself against
the jolt she knew would come, and did.

"Friends."

Twenty-Three

For the next two weeks, Christian and Lauren didn't see much of each other. Outside of meetings or the occasional room or hallway encounter, she was MIA, busy working on the concert, she'd said when asked.

But Christian knew that it was more than that. Whenever they met she was polite, poised and professional. She laughed when he joked with her and smiled on cue. No one could have accused her of being anything less than a standout, the kind of person any corporation or organization would be lucky to have working on their team. But he knew something was missing when he came around. Desire. Heat. He found himself remembering how they blazed in the throes of passion, found himself wanting to experience it again. But was it fair to reopen a door that he'd closed, especially for a brief visit instead of a longtime stay?

It wasn't fair to her. He knew this. But it didn't change

the fact that he wanted her, that without the real Lauren, all of her, days weren't as bright as they used to be and nights were much too long.

After wrestling with his thoughts and feelings a couple more days, he called his father.

"Morning, son."

"Good morning, Dad. Have you left for the office?"

"I'm not going in today."

"Everything okay?" Christian asked.

"More than fine. Now that you're president, I'm a thumb twiddler. Promoting you pushed me right out of a job."

"That's such a crock."

"But it made you feel good, didn't it?"

"A little bit." Christian headed toward the shower. "Is it okay to stop by before heading into the city? I've got a situation and could use your advice."

"I'll be here."

A short time later, he pulled his Bentley into the circular drive. Lauren's reaction to it had convinced him to buy it. If things worked out the way his mind had been headed, maybe he'd buy her one, too. Just beyond the foyer, he ran into Sofia.

"Where's Dad?" he asked, after greeting her warmly.

"In his study, waiting on you."

"Thanks, Sofia."

"Chris?" He turned around. "Are you hungry?"

"I'll grab something when I get to the office."

"Gabe just made cinnamon rolls. They're still warm."

"How can I say no to Gabe's gooey rolls?"

"I'll bring it down," Sofia said, smiling. "With milk."

Christian reached his father's study and after a light tap, opened the door. Where the rest of the house mainly had Victoria's aesthetic, this room was pure Nicholas

Breedlove. Christian took it all in as he crossed over to where his father sat on a love seat by a corner fireplace. The dark walnut walls, floor-to-ceiling bookshelves, rich leathers, antique desks and tables radiated pure masculine elegance.

Nicholas's dedication to family was evident in a grouping of portraits—him and Victoria, all of the sons. A small one of Nicholas's father, Jewel's first husband Bobby, and his group, the Soul Smokers. And Christian's favorite, the only one in color, of Nicholas's mother—their grandmother Jewel—which was prominently displayed in a rectangular gilded frame. She was at the center of a line of showgirls, adorned in fishnet stockings and sequins, with a feather headpiece at least three feet tall. He remembered visiting her home as a boy. Even then, in her fifties and sixties, no one could tell Christian that his grandmother wasn't a star!

In the boardroom Nicholas was all Rolex and Armani but here, in the study on his vast estate, one caught a glimpse of the foundation at the base of the man. His foundation was family, and owning one's own.

"What's going on, Pops?" Christian asked, settling down in a chair.

"That's what I'm about to find out," Nicholas said.

"Sofia's bringing in cinnamon rolls, just so you know."

Nicholas patted his stomach. "I've got a brand-new tuxedo for the next charity ball. That cummerbund has got to lie flat."

Christian nodded, totally understanding. He got all of his style from his father. But he hadn't come by to talk about fashion. And not having much time, he got right to the point.

"How did you know Mom was the one?"

Nicholas's eyebrows rose in obvious surprise. "Whoa, that wasn't the question I expected."

"Thought this was going to be about work?"

"Why, yes, I did, son. Don't mind your asking, but can I ask you something first?" Christian nodded. "Is this about Lauren?"

"It is."

There was a light knock at the door and once given permission to enter, Sofia brought in a tray of rolls and wheeled it over to where Christian sat. The smell of cinnamon, sugar and butter wafted under his nose. His stomach growled in delight.

"I brought coffee and tea, along with the milk."

"Thanks, Sofia," Christian said. "You're the best."

He reached for a saucer, picked up a roll and took a hefty bite. "This should be illegal," he said around the mouthful.

"For me, right now, it is," Nicholas replied.

Christian took a couple more bites before reaching for one of a stack of linen napkins, dipping it in a small crystal bowl filled with water and wiping his hands. "When Mom hired Lauren, I didn't remember that we'd met before."

"I don't know why you didn't. Faye and Vic have been friends for over twenty-five years."

"Lauren reminded me that it was her older sister Renee that I'd checked out."

Nicholas smiled, nodded. "Time brings about a change. She's a beautiful woman. But then, I'd imagine that's why you're here."

"Ah, Dad. I don't know what to do. We became close during that first trip to Africa and dated a couple times once we returned. But then she decided that mixing business with pleasure wasn't the best idea."

"Sounds like somebody I know," Nicholas replied, with a pointed stare toward Christian.

"All right, I admit to sharing that same viewpoint. I agreed with her, especially given that her mom and mine were friends."

"So what's the problem, she wants more now?"

"She did, but I messed it up."

"How?"

Christian stood and slowly paced the room. "By not being able to get over what happened. That's not exactly what I told her, though what I did share was the truth as well."

"Which was?"

"That perception is everything and that considering the fake marriage scandal, I wasn't sure dating her wouldn't mar the CANN image, have the public more focused on my private life than the next public offering.

"But that was only part of it. The other part is that she lied, big-time. I know there was a reason. I know it went further than she intended. I know she came clean. Intellectually, I get all that. I've forgiven her. But Dad, I just can't seem to forget."

"Did you tell her that?"

"At one point I did, right after reading the blog. She wasn't happy and not long ago came straight out with what she desired…for us to be together." Christian ran a hand through his curls and plopped down in a chair.

"Then I'm not sure I get your dilemma, son. According to Vic, Lauren is by far the best assistant she's ever had. Just the other day she told me that she could resign tomorrow and feel totally confident in her ability to lead the foundation on her own. Is she not producing the same level of work with the Island project? Is her attention to the gala interfering with what you need?"

"Not in the office," Christian mumbled.

Nicholas leaned against the back of his chair. "Earlier, you asked what it was about your mama that made me know that she was the one. It's when I started to think more about her than I did about any other woman, or even the business. It's when I started feeling lonely whenever she wasn't around. Let me tell you something, Christian. All the money in the world doesn't compare to the right woman warming the other side of your bed. You hear me?"

"I hear you, Dad. Thanks."

Christian gave Nicholas a hug and headed toward the door.

"It's good that you hear me," Nicholas said. "But the real question is, what are you going to do about it?"

It was a fair question, Christian thought as he headed to the car. He was determined to figure out the answer.

Twenty-Four

Lauren felt like pinching herself to make sure she wasn't dreaming. Partly because in preparing for the concert she'd gone nonstop, and sleepwalking was a real possibility. But mostly because her entire family would be attending before they continued to California for a long-overdue visit with some of their West Coast friends. Even Renee and hubby Thomas, always tied to their children, had left them with a sitter to spend some alone time in Sin City.

Lauren had balked at Victoria's suggestion that they all stay at the CANN but then she pulled the "it's my gift to Faye" trump card, putting her parents, sister and brother-in-law into a two-bedroom suite.

Lauren was staying at the CANN, too, along with most of the Breedloves. The concert and dance finished at twelve, but a private party for VIP guests would likely last well into the night. Staying there only made sense. As she sat perfectly still, letting the makeup artist Frankie had insisted on getting for her work her magic, Lauren thought of a third reason the night felt like a fairy tale. Her gorgeous couture gown, a gift from London and Ace, which was part of his latest HER collection.

As the makeup artist was finishing up, there was a knock at the door. One of the assistants went to open the door. It was Frankie, his pose regal, as he leaned on the jamb.

"The party can start now, darling," he cooed. "Fabulosity has arrived!"

He floated in on beaded Louboutins, his long legs clad in sequined skinny pants, paired with a feathery top and long drop earrings. His makeup was perfection and his hair had been cut, gelled and slicked back. He was drop-dead beautiful, and Lauren told him so.

"Please go and check on the rooms for the silent auction. Make sure all of the tablets are set, working, with styli and paper backup below. I feel fairly confident with the team we've assembled but with the extravagant donations we've received, we can't take any chances."

"I'm already all over it, girlfriend. The proceeds from tonight are going to be huge!"

There were collector's items being auctioned of Las Vegas greats—from Liberace, Jerry Lewis and the famous Rat Pack to more current headliners like Jennifer Lopez and Celine Dion. In an act of total selflessness, London donated her wedding dress. The bidding started at $250,000. Two interested parties had already phoned in.

A quick look at the clock said she needed to hurry. On cue, the hairstylist put down the rattail comb she'd been using to arrange Lauren's curls. Her hair had been pulled up and piled high into a burst of curls on top of her head. After viewing her jewelry she'd decided none was appropriate to go with the masterpiece Ace had designed. The dress alone would have to be enough.

Now it was time to become Cinderella. Lauren carefully stepped into the skirt, layers of deep red silk organza and gold tulle. She held her breath as the corset was laced, and figured the next time she breathed would be sometime tomorrow. Shimmering crystals accented the waist even more, and a boatneck bodice showed just the right amount of cleavage. After stepping into red satin pumps, she looked into the mirror. Indeed, she looked on her way to a ball. All she needed was a prince to complete the tableau.

There was a knock at the door.

"What has Frankie forgotten now?" Lauren asked the room. Although she'd given her family the suite number. It might be Renee.

It wasn't Renee. It wasn't family. It was her prince. *Christian.*

He stepped inside the door and stopped, his eyes drinking her in like a camel gearing up for a trek through the Mojave. Little did she know but her eyes mirrored his as she took in the deep red velvet tuxedo jacket, made more striking by being paired with a black shirt and slacks. His eyes caught and held hers, and she could swear the earth tilted. Everyone, everything in the room disappeared. Her heartbeat increased. She felt light-headed. Either the boning in the corset had cut through her windpipe or this sister was falling even deeper in love!

Seconds passed, and neither spoke. And yet an entire conversation passed through their eyes.

Yes. Me, too. Later. Can't wait!

"… Lauren!"

Someone was calling her. The name cut through a haze of emotions, softly at first and then louder.

She gave her head a slight shake to pull it together. The stylists had been forgotten. "Huh, um, what?"

"Do you need us for anything further?"

"No, but my family might." She gave them the suite number. "I'll let them know you're on the way."

The group scurried away, as though feeling like interlopers, suddenly unwelcome. Christian's eyes never left Lauren's as the door clicked in place.

"Hi," Lauren said shyly.

Christian visibly swallowed. "You take my breath away."

"I know the feeling. You look—" she licked her lips without meaning to do it "—really good."

"It's from the HIS collection."

"And this is HER."

"Ace did his thing with the summer line."

"Oh, I almost forgot. My family. The team. Let me call and give them a heads-up."

Lauren walked over to where her phone sat on the dining room table, next to a square gold clutch. After alerting her mom to the glam squad's arrival, she turned back to Christian.

"Shall we go down, then? I assume you're here as my escort?"

Slowly walking toward her, Christian said, "That's only one of many reasons why I'm here."

He stopped mere inches from her face. "The other is to give you this."

So caught up in his gaze, Lauren hadn't seen the box he held. Now she did, and looked at him again.

"What is this?"

"A peace offering."

"For what?"

"For telling you no when I should have said yes."

"Christian, I…"

"Shh." He placed a finger on her lips. "Let's talk later. For now we have a beautiful concert and a wonderful dance to enjoy."

Still staring at him, she lifted the lid and revealed another box inside, silver, with intricate designs. She let the cardboard box fall to the floor as she slowly lifted the silver box lid.

Her mouth dropped.

"No."

Christian chuckled. "What do you mean, no?"

"No, Christian! These can't be for me."

"They're absolutely for you, and now that I've seen how you're wearing that dress, baby, this present is perfect."

"They're beautiful," Lauren said, tearing up. "I've never…thank you."

"You're welcome. Here, you handle the earrings. I'll help with this."

Lauren turned, felt the coolness of the gem against her warm skin as he clasped the teardrop yellow diamond held by a thin gold chain. She put on the matching earrings and looked in the mirror. Now her ensemble was complete.

She looked at her watch. "I've got to go."

"Don't throw away that box. There's something else in there."

Lauren reached for the box and saw what lay at the bottom, what had been hidden by the intricately designed box that held the jewels. A hotel card key…to Christian's private suite.

He didn't know if she'd show, but Christian made the obligatory rounds at the VIP party, sent Lauren a text and then slipped out as quickly as he could. He entered the suite and looked around. His butler had staged the room to perfection, had followed every instruction to the letter. The candles, rose petals, champagne perfectly chilled, food flown in from Rome and Djibouti.

It had been so long since he'd been nervous about anything that at first he didn't recognize the feeling. Once he did he walked over to the bar, poured a finger of scotch and knocked it back. He walked over to the wall panel and pushed a few buttons. The soft sounds of neo soul floated across the room. Fifteen minutes passed, and then fifteen minutes more. He took off his jacket. Ten more minutes went by. Christian finally got the message. She wasn't coming. He walked into the bedroom, eased out of his shoes, and heard the soft *click* of the lock.

His heart thudded against his chest. There was another reaction, several inches below, as his sex twitched with anticipation. He walked into the living room. Lauren stood still, staring. She looked ethereal, like a goddess, the beads glittering, candles flickering off her golden skin. He walked over and pulled her into his arms.

"Thank you," he whispered.

He stepped back. She looked around. "This place looks amazing."

"It's all for you. Can I get you something to drink or eat? I've got some special dishes I think you'd like."

"Maybe later," she said softly. She perched on the sofa arm and slid off her pumps. "Right now I'd very much love it if you'd assuage another appetite."

Christian didn't need to be told twice. He pulled her up, turned her around and undressed her, everything but her thong, right there in the living room. While she was still standing he went to his knees, gently spread her legs and pressed his mouth against her heat. As his tongue snaked its way under the thong's silky fabric, his fingers splayed her cheeks and teased the star of her moon. Lauren groaned and joined him on the floor, using the $20,000 dress she'd just worn as a cushion against the cool marble.

Christian covered her naked body with his fully clothed one, took her face in his hands and kissed her deeply, her essence like nectar as he licked, nipped and teased. He stopped just long enough to pull off his shirt. As he worked with the buttons, Lauren handled his belt, button and zipper, and pushed down slacks and boxers in one fell swoop. It was a take-charge move that said "I want you now." The plans for a slow seduction went out the window. He reached for the condom in his slacks, rolled it on, and slid home.

Coming together again was heavenly. For a moment they lay still, barely breathing. He basked in the feeling of being fully sheathed inside her, of feeling the muscles of her inner walls flex and tighten, heightening his desire beyond what he thought possible. He eased out to the tip and sank in again slowly, deeply, smiling as the increased friction made her moan. He increased the pace—plunging, thrusting, squeezing, grinding—branding every part of her insides with his hot iron. He made love until a thin sheen of sweat covered his body and still, he could not get enough. His tongue and hands were everywhere. No part of her body, no crevice, no cavern, was left untouched. He poured himself into her, body and soul, and his mind whispered… *I love you.*

After the second orgasm and a leisurely shower, round two began and Lauren returned the favor. She licked and tickled his long, thick shaft, savored his tip, followed the line of hair with her tongue and drove him wild when she pulled him inside her warm, wet mouth. Over and over, until the sun rose. Until there were tears, as both of them recognized and acknowledged that what started as lust had deepened to a soul-mate love. They heated the food and conversed about trivial, mundane things. No one talked about the past. No one talked about the future, although later they'd realize that at this time they both saw the other in it. For right now, however, they only focused on the present, and each other.

Twenty-Five

The weeks between Memorial Day and the Fourth of July passed by in a blur of love, laughter, family and fun. Lauren and Christian spent quality time with Renee and Thomas, and dazzled them by scoring tickets to some of the best shows in Las Vegas—Cirque du Soleil and front-row seats to Criss Angel and MJ Live.

Afterward, Lauren traveled to California with her parents and marveled at the change in her dad. Or was it her just seeing him differently? Either way he seemed happier, his spirit much lighter. He still owed Gerald Miller a boatload of money, but hearing her dad's hearty laugh at a warm-up comedian made Lauren feel that the worst may indeed be behind them.

Paul and Faye came back for the Fourth of July celebration. Victoria had insisted on it, and on them staying in one of the guesthouses on the estate where the party was held. Thousands of mini lights—red, white and blue—were strung around and between three large white tents, with paths of slate laid between them, perfectly smooth and evenly laid in order to accommodate the Choo, Blahnik and Louboutin heels that would walk over them.

The best foods had been flown in from around the world, along with several renowned chefs in charge of a menu featuring Breedlove beef, Maine lobster, Alaskan salmon, Nova Scotia bluefin tuna and organic everything. Not a hot dog or potato chip in sight. One tent had been arranged with intimate seating for the one hundred or so guests who'd been invited. The third tent held additional seating, a lit dance floor and a massive bar that would attract a crowd all night.

Christian and Lauren arrived, hand in hand, a standout couple among a crowd of jewels. They spotted their parents at about the same time, sitting at a round table of ten, chatting with another couple and among each other. The lovers headed that way.

"Don't they make the cutest couple?" Victoria exclaimed after pleasantries. "And can you imagine their babies?"

"Victoria!"

"What?" Victoria held her ground while taking in Lauren's shocked expression. "You do know that's the end result of…hand-holding."

The table chuckled. Lauren swore her dad blushed.

"Sit down, you two," Nicholas said.

"Yes, do sit," Victoria said. "We have news to share."

Christian pulled out a chair for Lauren and sat down beside her.

"More specifically, Paul and Faye have news."

Lauren looked at her mom, then her dad.

"I wouldn't call it news, exactly," Faye began, her eyes

twinkling. "But your dad and I have been talking this week about how much we love Las Vegas. Years ago we joked about moving here when we retire and—"

"What?" Lauren's screech attracted more than one head turn. Who was this adventurous couple before her and what had happened to her parents?

"When did these conversations happen, because I've never heard the two of you talk about moving anywhere. In fact, Dad, you told me once that you were fine with coming to visit wherever I am but for you Maryland would always be home."

"I've learned that one should never say never," Paul said. "Life happens, things change, and so can perspectives. Sometimes we get so caught up in the year-in, year-out routine that we don't take the time to consider something different."

"And now you're considering a move across country? Okay, Mom." Lauren turned her attention to Faye. "I can totally imagine you wanting to move here. How did you bribe him?"

"That would be me," Nicholas said, raising his hand. "With CANN, there'll be major expansion over the next ten years and along with that the need for an increased workforce. We're always looking for skilled, dedicated people to join the team and considering the person you are, a talented force with creative ideas that are ingenious and progressive, I figure Paul had at least a little influence in how you turned out, and that's amazing."

"Nothing's official," Paul said. "I'd have to convince Gerald to let me go and then help find a suitable replacement."

"The truth, dear," Victoria continued, "is that this is all one big conspiracy to keep you here. The foundation is flourishing, the philanthropists love you, and so does everyone who works there. So with only a short time until your contract expires, we've had to put our heads together and work really fast."

It wasn't often that Lauren was speechless, but now was one of those times. She'd never been a weepy woman, either, but right now she could flat out boo-hoo. Looking between her mom and dad, they seemed so happy! And for the dad who not very ago lost his reputation, almost his freedom, and had been ready to resign, a job opportunity? Who knew?

"I really don't know what to say. It's not often my parents shock me, but I didn't see this coming.

"I know the holiday is over but you know what? This is truly a special gift and whether or not I stay past the contract, Nicholas, thank you. Despite everything that happened, when it comes to finances, you really couldn't hire anyone better than Dad."

Lauren waved over a waiter carrying champagne flutes. "It's time for a toast, guys." Christian reached for a flute as the parents raised their glasses. "To fateful endings, new beginnings and wonderful, amazing, astounding friends."

"I know I'm all that," Nicholas deadpanned. "But what about Vic?"

"On that note," Christian said with a laugh, pulling up Lauren, "I think it's time for us to hit the dance floor and get our party on."

"Don't make me have to hunt you down for my kiss of independence," Victoria chided.

"Are you kidding? You're my good-luck charm, Mom," Christian said. "I'll find you wherever you are."

As they headed toward the dance floor, Christian reached for Lauren's hand. He squeezed it and raised it to his lips. Their eyes met. He winked. A smile coasted from her face to his, lifted and brightened at an unspoken message of love, one that changed the atmosphere ever so slightly.

For years, he'd brought women to this annual gala, the brightest, most beautiful, rich, famous, all of the above. But he'd never felt that he was attending with the right one, the forever one…until now.

They reached the dance floor and as if on cue, the music shifted to a slow song. He slid his hand around Lauren's waist and pulled her into his arms.

"You're pretty amazing," Lauren whispered, sliding her hand across his butt. "Did you know that?"

"It never hurts to have the fact confirmed," he said.

Upon hearing those words, Christian's manhood swelled. He smiled, revealing a heart containing a giddy happiness he'd never felt before, exposing a soul reveling in complete contentment. It made him more convinced than ever that whatever happened, tonight was exactly how life was supposed to be.

"So are you going to tell me?"

Christian twirled her on the dance floor. "Tell you what?"

"How you talked your dad into hiring mine."

"That was all Nicholas. Nothing about me."

"I find that hard to believe."

Christian shrugged. "It's true. Besides, you heard my mom explain what this is really about. They're trying to keep you."

"And you have nothing to do with that, either?"

"Nothing about me."

They settled into the dance and the night, mingling with employees, patrons and friends, and taking advantage of line dances to boogie with everyone. By eleven o'clock the twins were feeling no pain and in a move right out of the movies, brought twins as their dates. Adam sat with a harem, literally, clustered together at a table for ten, nine beautiful women and him.

They ate, drank, partied down, and as day turned to night, he kept his promise and made his way toward the family. They all gathered in the open area, ready for the fireworks. Amid a flurry of colorful, fiery explosions, Christian turned to Lauren. "This is pretty impressive, but you're all the firecracker I need. I love you, babe."

"I love you, too."

The kiss was soft, teasing, a quick swirl of tongue before they ended it, shared a heartfelt embrace and hurried over to the Breedlove tables to watch the fireworks show. Amid the rockets' red glare and Roman candles bursting in the air, there were two people who were ready to give up their independence.

Noah and Nick assaulted their big brother. "Man, you're lame,"

"I thought you were going to go for the big one!" Noah said, frowning.

"What in the heck are you two talking about? For the rest of the night both of you should just say no."

"We're talking about the pro-pro, bro."

"The diamond ring, the knee bend thing. What are you going to do? Let a good one get away?"

Christian was amused, and touched, at the knuckle-heads' banter. They must have really liked Lauren, as they'd never given two hoots about his women before. They needn't worry. Christian had no intention of letting Lauren leave Las Vegas. Even now, a ring design that he'd worked on with Ace was in the hands of a jeweler to the stars. He wanted the ring to be original, like Lauren, one of a kind.

As for asking Lauren to be his wife? That would be a moment not shared with the masses. He lived enough of his life in the spotlight, and with the expansion of CANN that would happen even more. When the time came to declare his forever love, Christian had a plan. He would offer up a private proposal, for her ears alone. And Lauren's answer would be for just the two of them.

All she had to say was yes.

* * * * *

#2653 NEED ME, COWBOY
Copper Ridge • by Maisey Yates
Unfairly labeled by his family's dark reputation, brooding rancher Levi Tucker is done playing by the rules. He demands a new mansion designed by famous architect Faith Grayson, an innocent beauty he would only corrupt...but he *must* have her.

#2654 WILD RIDE RANCHER
Texas Cattleman's Club: Houston • by Maureen Child
Rancher Liam Morrow doesn't trust rich beauty Chloe Hemsworth *or* want to deal with her new business. But when they're trapped by a flash flood, heated debates turn into a wild affair. For the next two weeks, can she prove him wrong without falling for him?

#2655 TEMPORARY TO TEMPTED
The Bachelor Pact • by Jessica Lemmon
Andrea *really* regrets bribing a hot stranger to be her fake wedding date... especially because he's her new boss! But Gage offers a deal: he'll do it in exchange for her not quitting. As long as love isn't involved, he's game...except he can't resist her!

#2656 HIS FOR ONE NIGHT
First Family of Rodeo • by Sarah M. Anderson
When a surprise reunion leads to a one-night stand with Nashville sweetheart Brooke, Flash wants to turn one night into more... But when the rodeo star learns she's been hiding his child, can he trust her, especially when he's made big mistakes of his own?

#2657 ENGAGING THE ENEMY
The Bourbon Brothers • by Reese Ryan
Sexy Parker Abbott wants *more* of her family's land? Kayleigh Jemison refuses—unless he pays double *and* plays her fake boyfriend to trick her ex. Money is no problem, but can he afford desiring the beautiful woman who hates everything his family represents?

#2658 VENGEFUL VOWS
Marriage at First Sight • by Yvonne Lindsay
Peyton wants revenge on Galen's family. And she'll get it through an arranged marriage between them. But Galen is not what she expected, and soon she's sharing his bed and his life...until secrets come to light that will change everything!

Get 4 FREE REWARDS!

We'll send you 2 FREE Books plus 2 FREE Mystery Gifts.

Harlequin® Desire books feature heroes who have it all: wealth, status, incredible good looks... everything but the right woman.

FREE
Value Over
$20

YES! Please send me 2 FREE Harlequin® Desire novels and my 2 FREE gifts (gifts are worth about $10 retail). After receiving them, if I don't wish to receive any more books, I can return the shipping statement marked "cancel." If I don't cancel, I will receive 6 brand-new novels every month and be billed just $4.55 per book in the U.S. or $5.24 per book in Canada. That's a savings of at least 13% off the cover price! It's quite a bargain! Shipping and handling is just 50¢ per book in the U.S. and 75¢ per book in Canada.* I understand that accepting the 2 free books and gifts places me under no obligation to buy anything. I can always return a shipment and cancel at any time. The free books and gifts are mine to keep no matter what I decide.

225/326 HDN GMYU

Name (please print)

Address   Apt. #

City   State/Province   Zip/Postal Code

Mail to the **Reader Service:**
IN U.S.A.: P.O. Box 1341, Buffalo, NY 14240-8531
IN CANADA: P.O. Box 603, Fort Erie, Ontario L2A 5X3

Want to try 2 free books from another series? Call 1-800-873-8635 or visit www.ReaderService.com.

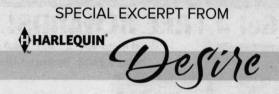
Faith had designed buildings that had changed skylines, and she'd done homes for the rich and the famous.

Levi Tucker was something else. He was infamous.

The self-made millionaire who had spent the past five years in prison and was now digging his way back…

He wanted her. And yeah, it interested her.

She let out a long, slow breath as she rounded the final curve on the mountain driveway, the vacant lot coming into view. But it wasn't the lot, or the scenery surrounding it, that stood out in her vision first and foremost. No, it was the man, with his hands shoved into the pockets of his battered jeans, worn cowboy boots on his feet. He had on a black T-shirt, in spite of the morning chill, and a black cowboy hat was pressed firmly on his head.

She had researched him, obviously. She knew what he looked like, but she supposed she hadn't had a sense of…the scale of him.

Strange, because she was usually pretty good at picking up on those kinds of things in photographs.

And yet, she had not been able to accurately form a picture of the man in her mind. And when she got out of the car, she was struck by the way he seemed to fill this vast, empty space.

That also didn't make any sense.

He was big. Over six feet and with broad shoulders, but he didn't fill this space. Not literally.

But she could feel his presence as soon as the cold air wrapped itself around her body upon exiting the car.

And when his ice-blue eyes connected with hers, she drew in a breath. She was certain he filled her lungs, too.

Because that air no longer felt cold. It felt hot. Impossibly so.

Because those blue eyes burned with something.

Rage. Anger.

Not at her—in fact, his expression seemed almost friendly.

But there was something simmering beneath the surface…and it had touched her already.

Don't miss what happens next!
Need Me, Cowboy
by New York Times *bestselling author Maisey Yates.*

Available April 2019 wherever
Harlequin® Desire books and ebooks are sold.

www.Harlequin.com

Love Harlequin romance?

DISCOVER.

Be the first to find out about promotions, news and exclusive content!

 Facebook.com/HarlequinBooks

 Twitter.com/HarlequinBooks

Instagram.com/HarlequinBooks

Pinterest.com/HarlequinBooks

ReaderService.com

EXPLORE.

Sign up for the Harlequin e-newsletter and download a free book from any series at **TryHarlequin.com.**

CONNECT.

Join our Harlequin community to share your thoughts and connect with other romance readers!
Facebook.com/groups/HarlequinConnection

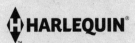

**ROMANCE WHEN
YOU NEED IT**

HSOCIAL2018